I0592563

KISS KILL

BOOK 1 - THE GIRL IN THE BOOK SERIES

DAN NOBLE

Illustrated by
THE COVER COLLECTION

DB CO.

You don't know how you got here
You just know you want out.
—U2, "Hold Me, Thrill Me, Kiss Me, Kill Me"

1

ERIN

You want to hear what happened to my girl. I understand. It's impossible to believe a thing like that could happen, so you want to hear about it over and over and over, but the truth is that no matter how many times you focus on the minute details, put it all together in a big picture, step back, and then sharpen your take, you're never going to know anything that makes sense of the thing. It happened, and we should all move on, or else off ourselves. But I couldn't possibly say that. People don't like coincidences and plain bad luck. They want reasons, to make sense of things. I can certainly understand that.

It is not new to me, this feeling of being a plus-one. My husband is an important so-and-so. He is brave and good and cares about the rights and safety of people. He is the kind of person who makes you look in the mirror and say, Why the hell am I so worried about failing as a person/whether there will ever be another opportunity to feel good about another day beginning/if my speech is often accelerated and slightly hysterical, sounding as if I've drunk one too many coffees? Because there are people out there who exist on rice—when they can get it, that is—and who have lost their legs and family members to land mines and now have to swindle and connive to get enough to pay for a piece of plywood to put over their head for a shelter. They don't have time to think about whether they like themselves. Losing merely one child is considered lucky.

The fact remains, now I am a plus-one in Olivia's story, and this is as it should be. Still, I am here, and as unpalatable as the following will sound to you, it sounds even more so to me: I would like to move on, and so I am taking myself to a small restaurant overlooking the ocean, with the express goal of sleeping with a man I have thrice seen go to this restaurant, sit at the bar, and not speak with anyone but the bartender. I have told my husband I am meeting a friend for dinner.

I kept it simple, which is what you're meant to do with lies. He didn't ask which friend. This is not surprising. Gav does not listen to me. He avoids looking at me because our daughter looked like me—with the olive eyes (*who ate the pimento?* he used to say) and the fuzzy, fine hair (though mine is not arranged in piggy tails or twisty snails—yes, these erstwhile adorable twists of phrase stay in your head when they have turned perverse and painful to hear; the brain is not our friend), and the heavy forward-leaning walk (*we've got places to go!* she and I used to say)—and I pretend not to notice, and in this way we are able to go to sleep at night and wake in the morning and smile at the air when he leaves for work each day.

But it's been nine years now, and I am not going to admit publicly to this terrible reality, which sounds obscene even to myself, but here it is: I want.

And I believe what I want is to live again. The activities I most often think about longingly are snorting in laughter and smiling naturally—and not just in private, or on the sly, when someone steps in shit or loses their cool at a supermarket cashier and drops the F-bomb.

I went last week and bought one of those full skirts with the pockets that look so elegant to me, and a fitted blouse that comes just to the waist of the skirt. The shop girl got so excited because she'd been trying to sell this look, and no one was ready for it, she said. I liked the sound of that for this occasion and enjoyed remembering the feeling of being fashion forward—a thing of simple sensory delight, so I bought everything she suggested—even the shoes and the earrings. She showed me, in a three-way mirror with light bulbs up the sides, how to twist my hair up in the new way—high, tight, but slightly imperfect. The Erin in that mirror was the Could Have Been Erin. It was so obvious that it got me thinking I must be on the right track.

I wore it all home, smiled slightly madly at the mailman, and then quickly ran upstairs to undress and wash my face and unpin and fluff out my hair. After that, I went into Olivia's room and tried to remember what it was like to be annoyed at her for not picking up her alphabet blocks the way I had told her to three times, to tell her she must sit on the top step for two and a half minutes and think about what she had done ("I'm *think*ing," she'd sing-song down the stairs while I tried not to laugh), to tell her she would not be able to watch *Ben and Holly's Little Kingdom* if she didn't eat her cheese sandwich (not the crusts, obviously).

I could remember, but I couldn't recreate the lip-curling irritation those moments used to rouse. What was so trying about a child not eating her cheese sandwich? It was Jarlsberg, for crying out loud; I never would have *looked* at Jarlsberg when I was that age. The guilt is unsettling, usually, but this time, it settled—like a dog hair in my water glass that I couldn't fish out —tangible, locatable, out of place. I took this as proof; I was doing the right thing. Sure, I might continue to gag on it, but a gag, I could handle.

I didn't go that Friday. Instead I waited until the next one, in case I wanted to change my mind, a thought which never once did I entertain. There was a parking space right in front, and payment was not required for the meter, as it was after six. This was a typical North Queensland pub, but cleaned up and renovated, so that it had become slightly bland, but in turn had clean toilets and nice-enough brick oven pizzas.

I walked up to the barman, without scanning to look for The Man, and asked for a Tom Collins. Now, I had no idea what was in a Tom Collins, but I didn't want to do anything that came naturally to me. I stirred the cherry-orange skewered toothpick regretfully, but on my tongue the drink was sweeter than I'd imagined; refreshing. *Refreshing refreshing refreshing.* God, I hate that word; *it's an ad for a word, it's not an actual word* is something I used to say at dinner parties when there was nothing else to go for.

Gav doesn't expect me to go to dinner parties anymore, and it was a relief now—because I wouldn't be instantly recognized here the way I once would have been when I was more social. If I was noticed at all, someone might think, I know her from *somewhere*. And though I was grateful for the increased degree of anonymity, I missed society, the careful costuming, the mysteriously confident self-deprecation. I was good at it. I had been lucky. Post career stall-out, mine had become a life of enjoyment, that rare thing I'd worked long and hard to attain.

But now I was a person who said *refreshing* and meant it. And this person just spied the man she was going to sleep with. He was wearing a Billabong T-shirt with an incomprehensible image on it that probably meant something to people who surf, but was lost on me. For all I knew, it was lost on him, and he was merely pretending to be amongst the knowing. For all I knew, he'd washed it a million times in a few weeks to make it look that old because it was cooler that way. Or he was wearing an old shirt because he didn't give a shit about what people thought, and the image had once been comprehensible, but had worn away in the important spots. Or it had been bought for him that way, and he'd never given it a thought.

It was surprisingly easy to make eye contact. An old song I remembered from the early wear-makeup-to-bed days with my husband, then boyfriend, was playing. I looked up, and bang. There were that surfing T-shirt wearer's eyes. They were kind and the skin around them sun slackened; but there was a vacuous quality to them that frightened me a little—and was exactly the reason I'd chosen him.

The punk song's purposely blasé base line worked its magic: I remembered this slightly condescending thrill of *getting it* and smiled—a real one produced by a happy thought. After wanting it all this time, I couldn't believe how shameful it felt. But it was too late. He had already taken the grin as an invitation and walked over.

"Can I buy you a beer?"

"But I'm drinking a Sav Blanc."

"Can I buy you a beer?"

"Are you saying that's all that's on offer?"

"Yes."

"Interesting."

"Is it?" There was the smell of a fresh shower on him.

"Very." I was halfway between running and completely throwing myself into this; there wasn't feeling and thought as much as the sense of having been thrown into the middle of the ocean and trying to survive.

"I'll take that as a yes."

"If you insist."

"No one said anything about insisting." This self-assurance would come off as a good thing in any other situation, but it's the worst look for a mourning mother—confident is not what people want to see. They want to see how terrible your pallor is, how timid the world has made you so they can ply you with pity-kindness, all the while trying not to look terrified that they might catch your bad luck before they bolt home, hug their kids, and thank God it hadn't happened to them.

"Two Four X Gold." An indiscreet nod from the young bartender said a lot. There was judgment there: old-man tastes that never change. My man must have been here plenty.

"Mmmm," I said, incredulous.

His look said he caught on but didn't care.

"Seen you here before."

"You have," I said. I didn't worry over the silence; it seemed nuanced, measured. We drank and watched two girls, indecently dressed, enter the bar. Always the same thought: if my daughter ever dressed like that . . .

"Live over this way?"

"Up in the big house, at the point."

"Ah." He took a long sip. Why had I said that? The plan was ruined, and I ought to have run; I'd sabotaged it purposely, hadn't I? Do I want to be that man? I imagined him thinking. The one who had an affair with *that woman*. But maybe it was more a general wondering about the kind of woman who comes on to a man when she lives in that kind of house and is married to an important so-and-so and should be lying in the dark, crying over Olivia. What had it ever been like to be anonymous? Clearly, I didn't want to recall.

"And you?"

"In the littlest house, as far from the point as you can get."

"Ah."

Silence.

"So what do you do with yourself . . . ?"

"Erin."

"Erin; I'm Mick."

"Nice to meet you, Micko. I . . . work as a waitress." I was as surprised as he was to hear it come out of my mouth.

He didn't ask where, only half-heartedly followed along with my obvious lie. "And how do you find that?"

I let out a horsey sigh. "Honestly? It's a fairly subtle art."

He laughed.

"No, really. It sounds silly; I know. But hear me out. Look—look at that girl with the short skirt standing at the far table, taking down that young family's order. Everyone's got this expectation at that table—I'm going to get that great barra with the herby crust; I'm really looking forward to their chips with the tarragon. So, she's got them already on a hook. Then it's the simplicity that gets me: take the order, pass it to the kitchen, retrieve the order; transaction complete. There's a beautiful symmetry to restaurant dining if you know how to see it. It's a time out; you can be anyone, but here—you all do the same thing. You eat your fish and chips and have a drink and pay your bill and look at the taped-up sign that says, 'tips,' ignore it, and then go home. The great equalizer." Did I really believe that? Was it actually simplistic, easy, or was it precisely the kind of simplicity that says everything if you just meditate on it long enough? What about all the people who couldn't afford to eat out, who didn't get any protein in their diets? Where was the equality for them? Again, the thought: losing one kid was considered lucky in those kinds of places—it was the ones who'd lost five, seven, who had it rough.

"Okay." His look said it all.

"Aren't you moved by my depth of vision?"

"Completely."

"You aren't very keen to impress."

"No."

He wasn't vacuous. He'd tricked me, too.

I wish I could say I was aroused; that there was a flicker of eroticism in our exchange. But I hadn't felt anything along those lines in a long time; I wasn't wearing sexy underwear—just the same style nude bra and panties I wore daily. If there was a strip of lace, it certainly wasn't designed to entice as much as soften. What passed between us wasn't inconsiderable, though.

The lights and music dulled twice—as if the power were about to go out. A chorus of *uh-oh* ensued, but everything returned to normal.

"And you? What do you do?"

"Does it matter?" Our looks challenged. What were we saying? My experiment had gone off the rails, and I should probably jump ship now. This was about more than a one-night stand; there was no turning back from a move like this.

Oh, stuff it. "It does. Turns out I'm not as slick as I'd thought."

"I could have told you that."

"Don't do that."

"What?"

"Shift over to this version of things without missing a beat."

"Apologies, but I *am* as slick as I thought."

I smiled. The sensation wasn't as painful this time. Besides, I'd done it in private, in the cloak of a dark closet nearly daily. I just had to, in the same way that tonight I just had to do this. "So what do we do now?"

"Eat something?" He gestured toward the dining room. "I hear the herb-crusted barra is great."

Our table was in a terrible spot—too close to the bar, and near a band setting up, already too loud during the sound check. The table was immaculate, though, as if it was loved, this ordinary thing. Exchanging smiles, we ordered the barra—his with baked potato, mine with salad. We were past the age when chips were tempting; they were a precursor to a bad belly and a couple extra kilos.

The second round of drinks arrived on their beer mats. Everything did seem to make sense. We sipped.

"Good band, this one."

"I can only imagine."

"No, you'll see."

The first song was a classic designed to make the crowd warm to the band. It worked. Everyone loves a sing-along. I found myself resistant to liking them; I didn't want him to be right. But in the familiar strums and riffs, we found our former selves (it wasn't just me) and scanned to see whether we'd been transported to those could-have-beens. There's a belligerent hope in musical memory, and it was in this toughness I mustered the strength to stay.

The band went right into a new song I recognized from the radio, but their rendition was arranged differently, slowly, thoughtfully. When it was through, I realized I'd disappeared into it. If I wanted to sleep with this man, why wasn't I doing it? I wasn't even flirting; where was all the smiling I'd planned on doing?

"So tell me something."

I took him where my brain had been lately. "Okay. Do you read?"

"That's more of a question." He'd somehow eaten all his fish and now lifted his fork to make some headway on the potatoes. "Yes, I read. History mostly."

"History; never can get at the whole truth, so take the best you can get at."

"Of course you gotta question everything, or you'll get fed all kinds of rubbish. So, you were saying?"

You sound like my husband, I nearly said. "I'm working up to it. Did you know novels—proper modern ones that we read today—only began to take shape when writers left the morality play setup and started to feature specific people, writing the stories autobiographically, as if the action was happening to them?"

"You really know how to turn a guy on."

"Really, I'm trying to answer your first question—honestly now. Hang on."

"You're not really a waitress? And I went ahead and took your tip on the barra."

"You know I'm not."

"Okay; thrill me."

"Archetypes, moral tales were what everyone wrote, not someone frying onions and stepping over a crack and hammering nails to make it feel real. But see? That change of perspective, and bam! An amazing way to open up unique experience to the world. And the magic of it is," I held up a finger in pause, "It's the specificity of the representation that truly began to tell stories that connected universally, because the more authentic the details, the more realistic the experience, and the reader could feel they were walking in the characters' shoes. I could think all day about the infinite narrative techniques novels use to recreate reality without *copying* it. It's so real that sometimes—sometimes—" The finger again; I used to use this finger all the time. People would say, *watch out, she's pulled out the finger!*

He ducked; I'll give old Micko that; he had a sense of humor. "You could nearly imagine you're living that life, or not so much living it, but that the experience aroused by reading those lives is the real life, while all of *this* doesn't matter at all." By the hand sweep, I'd lost him. I talked too much, too fast, and now I sounded manic. I could tell by the way he'd changed his posture that he thought I was a crazy woman who'd lost her mind when her daughter was "taken from her" (or insert other palatable way of saying the unpalatable). I took a sip, slowed my breath, my cadence. "I used to think how I could never imagine it, a life without novels. It would be impossible. But then something happened."

"Something happened." He knew. I obviously wanted him to: Why else would I have told him where I lived? Now he knew, just like everyone else. Ha ha, Erin!

"Yes, and then I never read a novel again."

"A punishment?"

"Sort of. And do you know what I learned?"

"That you were a creative sufferer?"

"No. That books—to people who love them—and movies and clothes and all that culture *is* actually important. Every bit as much as the moral or emotional, ethical or economical duties. It's how you live your life. And when you don't do any of it, your life has no framework to hang itself on. It just slumps on the floor like a dirty shirt."

"Like a dirty shirt."

"So, though I never thought so, writing is important. Some historians say that only the written-about things ever actually become part of history. If you don't write it, it didn't happen. Can you imagine?" Why was I speaking like a university lecturer? Why did I keep saying things I'd said I wouldn't? Maybe this was good; maybe this was the process I needed, but couldn't have predicted, couldn't have known until I was in the midst of it— this is why "pantsing" is always the best writing technique. I explained the term to him: when the research and characters in their scenes take you someplace you never could have predicted. You let yourself go and see where you're taken. Don't be fooled; it's the opposite of simple. There are complex brain processes going on here. Trust them, I explained. The more refined concepts of stories are out of reach until we find ourselves immersed in the world of the story—because meanings are not simple, conscious conceits: they are a complex maneuver of projection, linking, and blending. There's tons written on this, though people only ever want to know ridiculously simple things about books: what they're about. Why were these the things I spent my time thinking about? What I normally did wasn't thinking so much as *being* in that book world, with a mind that refused to know we'd completed the normal part of our lives. I'd gone so long without anyone to share it with, this exchange had become a sort of eruption. Lucky guy. "And so, we come to history. Your favorite."

"Did anyone ever tell you you think too much?"

"No, no. None of this makes much sense unless you know that I was a novelist and that I gave that up, too." No, I didn't give it up so much as it gave me up. All the popular cable television series stole my life and made it better. But back when I was living those lives, no one liked that kind of thing. And I didn't know how to write about it properly even if they had. I used circular sentences; I didn't know shit about simple language. I recall some serious abuse of em dashes. In others' work, I could spot *it*, and it could make me lie in bed all day weeping when some novelist I loved and loathed at the same time got it right, but it wasn't going to be me causing someone else such sweet distress. I wasn't good enough. And if I ever again heard about Mozart or Van Gogh not being appreciated until they died, I was going to spontaneously combust.

Yes, I think too much. That is probably part of the problem. People had always said that, but that was a different Erin; of this one's thoughts, I didn't know what people would make. Amazingly, I didn't care.

"Still, you might want to think about all this thinking. It seems to me you used to be a lot of things."

"This is something true, finally. And now?"

"And now?"

"Now I am sitting here with a man, telling him things he doesn't care to know."

"Would you like to come home with me?"

"No. I don't think I would."

"You sure?"

"No. Not exactly sure."

"Then you might be persuaded?"

"It would take a lot."

He looked at his watch. "It's already eight thirty."

Men here knew how to be men; the antidote to us. I'd give him that. I pictured myself beneath him, in my plainly elegant underwear, but I didn't like what I saw—breathing and pushing. What were we all grabbing at? I touch this man, he touches me, and then what? Why all the touching? Wasn't there any other way out? What do you want, Erin? You tried a life, and you failed. Okay, but what comes after that? I didn't want to die; I wanted to want to, but I just wasn't built that way. A higher power, or a religious epiphany; these things I could have clung to if they'd shown themselves, but what about when you can't get your smart-aleck girl back and there's just more? Every single day, the fucking sun in your eyes?

The waitress took Micko's empty plate while the guitarist was picking out a folksy, melancholy song I'd always liked. He ordered us another round. I wasn't much interested in my food, though it looked nice enough—salad that was more than a garnish, a fresh herby sauce in an old-fashioned fluted paper cup. My mobile rang while I was spearing a flake of fish.

"Gav." I could tell from the ringtone it was my husband. He often called me on his way home, though we never said much. I would listen to the ABC, rattling on to him until I could hear him pull in the drive.

I shouldn't have answered it; the thing to do was put it in my bag and continue on.

"Hello, Erin." There was Mark Colvin on the radio in the background, kindly and evenly enunciating his way through a terrifying story about people smugglers. The band finished with a fancy drum roll, and I panicked.

"I'll be home in a few minutes," I said. "Let me go because you know how I am, driving at night." He did. He knew this about me.

"Right-o. See you in twenty or so."

I knew Mick was looking at me. Obviously, he'd be wondering what in the world I was up to.

"What's all that noise I hear?"

"Noise? Sorry, I can't hear you; it's too loud. If you can hear me, I'll see you in twenty minutes." I disconnected the call.

Mick tried his best to look nonplussed, which only made him look plussed.

"I'm sorry," I said. "I don't know what I'm doing. I really have to go." I pulled out my wallet.

He clasped the wallet with a firm grip. "Don't you fucking dare."

Alone in the car outside the restaurant, I hauled out my notebook and furiously expunged every word in my head. Here it was: my conversation with Micko projecting into something before my eyes; the plan was working! I could feel myself smile. I didn't know what I was about to write before the marks shone on the page, and yet here they were! Something lovely, finally, happening to me. I did my best to allow myself to enjoy it. I was giddy when I heard the knock at the window. It was Micko.

At the red light just meters away, I saw Gav's car idling. I could hear the talkback from the cracked window. I felt guilt—waves of it.

"What are you doing?"

"Research," I said. The light across turned green. I watched Gav's car drive out of sight, feeling incredibly nauseous.

"Are you writing about what just happened between us?"

"Well, no. Yes. Okay, yes. I am."

"You looked like you enjoyed the writing more than the dinner."

"Ha ha."

"Seriously."

"I probably did."

"I'll try not to take that personally."

"I don't see why."

"Ouch."

"Can I ask you a question?"

"Are you going to write down my answer?"

"Probably."

"Right. So go ahead, I guess."

"Why are you still talking to me?"

"Honestly?"

"No. You should lie to me. In this polite, normal situation we find ourselves in, I don't think it would really be appropriate to be yourself."

"I see your point."

I blinked twice, wiggled my pen. I was having fun; weird, not-good-for-anybody fun. There. I said it.

"I haven't enjoyed myself this much in a long time."

"You have serious problems."

"*I* have serious problems?"

"I see your point."

It was a nice smile, that one. Genuine. A car's headlights illuminated the back of his head, like he could have been an angel, or a Christmas ornament—the classic kind that wasn't necessarily beautiful, but really pegged the spirit.

"Can I see you again?"

This was getting out of control. I had to shut it down.

"Why?"

"You make me think differently."

"Okay, yes. Yes you can."

2

ERIN

I have a confession. The motive I gave in the beginning is not exactly true. Yes, I want to smile and laugh, but that is not the only reason I did this. I could watch *10 Things I Hate About You* for this to happen (yes, it is still funny post Heath Ledger, though his character now reads as incredibly insightful). It still works. I've tried it. In fact, it worked so well that when I caught my teary, laughing face in the mirror, I went purple and turned it off. I could not bring myself to throw it in the trash.

I had heard of a woman in New York, who had managed to blur the lines between fiction and reality, who'd warped the natural order somehow. My research on this woman never brought up anything definitive. But she'd disappeared and there were claims by a mysteriously named Dr. P, that she'd managed to focus her mind's participation in a story to such a strong degree that she'd actually been physically absorbed into it. Given my guilt (however ridiculous) over having apparently written Olivia's death into reality, I'd become obsessed with the idea. This is not the kind of thing I would share with anyone.

Especially Gav. And mostly I didn't believe it, but lately, I could see how—in the right circumstances, with the right person—such a thing could, maybe happen.

And so what was I writing in my car after Micko drove off, and well beyond the twenty minutes in which I'd told Gav I'd see him at home? I am sure I should be ashamed to say I felt flushed from the thrill of the words rushing out from that peculiar place where they are generated. But rush they did. On the page, where I mused about what would happen to some fictional character in a similar situation to the one I'd just extricated myself from, sometime in the near future, "Ricko" asked me to meet him at his place, and then he told me he'd been thinking about me.

I could tell he wanted to have sex. There was the look that would lead to touching. He was close. There was a sense of something about to happen.

On the page, I was different than I would be if this had happened tonight—I wanted it too. I shifted my legs, arched my back. I was satisfied with the idea of my sexuality, the way I could please a man.

───

At this point, off the page, it was all very innocent. I lived; I felt inspired; I wrote. I liked the way the events had taken on their own momentum. Again, this pantsing—the story propelling me along. It was a thrill. I caught myself singing in the shower. Olivia used to do a bit with me about that, and I smiled to think of it. "Is that good singing?" I used to say. "No. It isn't." She meant it, too. Cheeky little thing.

And this week, at my computer, I took this bare-bones scene, and I made something where there was nothing—a story, a sympathy, an experience. I created events from thin air to happen to the character "Erika." I don't know what I expected—certainly not symmetry from page to life, nor a canceling out of what had happened with Olivia. I don't think I was deluded enough to believe I could make something happen because I strung together thoughts into letters, into words, into a narrative structure that made people feel they were experiencing something profound. It began as a story premise, sprung from who knows where, during the pantsing. Of course I did not believe anything would happen off the page. One could not write a thing and then make it happen. And yet, I spent the week writing with the strange feeling of something happening. And there were moments—lightning moments—when I had got it exactly right; I knew that I had. "Ha ha!" I bellowed, smacking the desktop. Fuck, it felt good.

In my favorite bit, I say to Micko, "Let's see if you know what I wrote that I wanted to have happen next." I don't know why I liked that bit, as it was simple. But it tested the way things could work. In what I wrote next, Erika liked the sex. But I knew in real life I would not. This part of me had been turned off.

I drank wine and coffee and left rings on the tempered glass and didn't wipe them off. The next morning, I walked over to check that they were really there, because my real life was beginning to feel unreal, so out of step with what it had been. Next time I saw him, I would tell Micko about my hypothesis, and he would find it tragic, and yet he would allow himself to be swept up in it because I'd made everything feel authentic, while bringing him along the wildest ride.

I had twenty-five pages by the time I saw Mick on the following Thursday. Each day, I'd put my laptop on the table outside and written from the second Gav left to the second he rang from his car in the evening. Mark Colvin. ISIS.

International Trade Agreement. Violence at Christmas Island. I didn't get inspiration from the view beyond my window; I liked the temperature—a bit cooler now, with a lively wind that required a ponytail to keep hair from flicking into my mouth and eyes. I didn't appreciate the sea outside my windows. I didn't see it; if I still made self-deprecating cocktail banter, I would have said it had become like a piece of plywood. I felt nothing—not even the rushing of waves had the slightest affect. I have come so far the other way, I don't understand why views do anything for anyone. It is not as if you walk away from a garden as a rose.

There was *vivre*, but no *joie*. I didn't feel "better" while I concocted an alternate reality of Mick and myself—one that sprung into being with the kind of boundless, buried inspiration that I know comes from the layers of experience wrapped around Olivia's death. I reserved feeling any specific kind of way about the wellspring. Perhaps *reserved* is the wrong word as it implies an effort, which was not the case.

But I made something. Which isn't to say there is a healing or satisfactory element to writing for me. It was not cathartic. I did not walk away as a garden rose. I did not walk away as anything other than a woman whose daughter—the one fond of wearing gumboots with ballet skirts—was smashed by a drone when she was posed hip-handed on the veranda, in the gumboots and a particularly threadbare tutu, painting a picture of her dadda eating blueberries (which he never did). Yes, this drone was doing something ridiculous—mapping shortcuts for pizza delivery routes—which, let's face it, in fiction, would add levity to a grim tale, but which in reality doesn't feel much different than any other kind of unreal loss. There was a little girl with a perpetual milk moustache in gumboots and a tutu, and now there is not.

The writing was a test. Looking back at this point, I believe I sensed where it would all end up, but I played along, let myself get swept away in the finale.

Off the page, Mick chose a more stylized place this time. It was the kind of place where young girls wear mature clothes and shoes they can't walk in. I knew some of our friends came here and I could have been spotted, but I went without suggesting an alternative. You have to allow characters to do what they will. The tension of possibly running into someone would make it all the more interesting. Besides, I secretly wondered what someone would do with information like that. It made for excellent conflict.

"So what are you really doing here?" he said, handing me a beer. The sip was more pleasurable than I expected; already, the brain creating new pathways—see? See all the things we're meant to do, most of which we never even consider?

Though I understood Mick already knew, I told him—via the canned two-sentence version—what happened to Olivia. I did not mention *10 Things I Hate About You*. I surprised myself by continuing on, in another, more truthful way. "The worst part is that I wrote a novel about this; a little girl gets killed accidentally in some way we don't find out in the story. It didn't even do well. And then it happened to my own daughter." The word *daughter* rang strangely in my mind and echoed there. "I am not superstitious. I know I did not make this happen. It is more that I am convinced of a link somewhere—a link between writing and living. It exists. It is difficult to explain to someone who does not write, but when you do—when you really get good at it and master the format, removing all the obstacles—the writing happens in the most passive way. You do not know where it is coming from. You do not make it come. You go about your life, absorb what you absorb, and you sit down, and this comes out. And then after, when it happened in real life, I knew—however grimly—I was onto something. So now I am testing it." I did not say that I am to blame. This is open for inter-pretation.

"And I am the test?"

"Yes."

"How do you know if you pass?"

I shrugged.

He grimaced, shaking his head until he was laughing.

I don't know why I continued to say these things to Mick. This was not part of the plan. Funny how sharing seems to come so naturally, breaking rank with other motives. I am not sure whether he believed me. As a bereaved parent, is it better to be crazy than to want to laugh? As soon as it came out, I liked the idea of him knowing. It was a kind of pantsing and just as exhil-arating. It didn't seem to matter if the writing bit or the real-life bit came first anymore, as if they'd melded together and I didn't know where one began and the other ended. A profound connection. Profound was the key. Mostly, though, I liked the idea of Olivia's death being more than a ridiculous anecdote that people began with, "Oh, you won't believe this!" She deserved to be immortalized, and not as the poster child for drone reform.

There was another element, too. Including Mick was almost like having a child; he believed me because he thought I was more intelligent than him. The same way I often get sucked into esoteric literary novels that stink, but I'm too afraid to say because I am terrified there is a small chance it might mean I just don't get it.

This wasn't a coincidence. I'd done my homework. "I know what you're thinking," I said. "But this isn't some kooky artist hogwash."

"You're wrong there: I never think the word *hogwash*."

I smiled; giggled a little. How could it be that this bizarre, incrementally dangerous experience could also be fun? Because stories are not straight lines. I repeated this phrase aloud. And then went on: "They are unfolded, linked, and experienced on any number of conceptual connections. They work because the mind is literary. This is not a new concept in neuroscience. We are wired to understand and link complex thoughts and concepts, memories and impressions to make sense of our world from infancy. The mind works in stories."

"The mind is a terrible thing to waste."

He ordered another two beers. I could feel the alcohol loosening the story from my mind. "So don't you think it's possible that there are connections we haven't made yet, simply because we don't know how?"

"Sure."

"You're a man of many words."

He smiled. People like it when they think you know them. Which is why he put his hand on the back of my neck and kissed me. It was thrilling in the way dream physicality is: indulging in the taboo—cheating in public in a town where your husband is in the paper every day! I shouldn't! And I am ashamed to say it was this bit that excited me. I tried to reason around the possibility I could be so simply base, but I was hyperaware of where we were and what we were doing, and my skin prickled with this before our lips even met. This is behavior I would be disgusted with in another person. I was not me.

See? I said while I was writing that you can't predict exactly what will happen: I *was* turned on. I wouldn't have thought it possible. And this is the bit that interests me—it's not a simple write X and Y happens. No, it's a delicious, rich, brocade of neurobiology that you have to encounter in all its complexity. And it was working. I had to see how far I could take it.

I made it happen. I had done the same with Olivia, so now I could hate that last little bit of myself I hadn't before. Freedom. Still, it is also true that I picked something easy to begin the test with. I'd known Micko was willing.

When our mouths parted, there was a moment of visual exchange—so close up in his liquid blue eyes—with no room for barriers. Is it real intimacy, the feeling this kind of looking imparts? Or is it an illusion, simply a product of physical proximity? Is there really any difference if the mind processes it the same? At the edge of that moment, just as my exhale completed, I was struck with the thought: imagine if this singular moment was *not* connected to any of those other particularities, if I were *not* trying to harness the power of the written word? Being locked in a moment, separate from any other, is a different kind of experiment—one that would surely end in failure, but the execution would be fantastic. Free in the true sense. I believe now that I had hoped this experiment would fail, so I could unburden myself of at least some of the guilt about Olivia—see what I've done! It is not possible to write something and magic it into reality. But here I was.

As a woman approaching her forties, there is no romance about groping a man in public. It is done behind closed doors, and this is precisely where we took ourselves once it got underway. On the way out, I don't think I was recognized by anyone. Though a pinky-blonde woman in flared pants did look familiar to me, I don't believe she was anyone who knew Gav. My mind imaged her at a register: Perhaps the pharmacy or supermarket? She could hardly be concerned with me. In fact, she didn't seem to notice me at all.

Mick's house was an old Queenslander, but not a nice one. It did not even have good bones, he said.

"Why would you pick a house like that?"

"To show I can make something out of nothing." Perhaps, his look said, we are not as different as you think.

It was methodical, the way Mick removed my clothing—

every single piece—and then pulled me to the sofa, where he laid me down and continued to kiss me in that way he had at the bar. Now it was the car ride that had increased the tension. I had watched the back of his head through his truck's rear window as I followed him here and thought, I know the man whose head that is. I have just kissed him. I thought of the garden rose metaphor. What was so potent about this feeling? It had been only two sets of lips upon each other. I didn't put too much stock in the similarities in my real and fictionalized reactions, because in the car, I got to thinking, this could be the power of suggestion. I needed a more concrete predictor test. Something Mick would do, something out of my head and hands. I thought over my passages. The words I put in his mouth.

"We shouldn't, Erika darling," he whispered into the apple of my cheek.

Some might say Micko and I would have had sex regardless of whether I wrote about it beforehand. But what about the way he twirled my hair, the way he said, "Erin, doll." It is exceedingly similar to "Erika, darling," is it not? The way he whispered not just in my ear, but on me, into my skin, "We shouldn't."

The act itself did not bring me to orgasm, but I trembled as I felt the tip of him part me. My eyes closed, and I did feel, for that moment, that I was disconnected from the rest of it—Olivia, Gav, the experiment, the guilt, everything. It was so simply satisfying and peaceful that I thought, after, perhaps I had overthought it. Maybe I *could* disconnect myself from everything and just be this. Was that hope? When it was over, he rolled over onto the floor, sighing profoundly. I giggled.

3

MICK

"This old clunker doesn't even have good bones," I said to her.

"Why would you pick a house like that?" she'd asked me.

It was slick, I thought, the way I said I wanted to show I could make something out of nothing. The truth was, it was cheap, and I knew I could do anything with a house—or with anything else, for that matter. I knew she would see it as a common link between us; obviously her romantic side got the better of her. She couldn't help hoping, not that I could blame her. In fact, it's what attracted me. If a woman could still be looking to pull through after what she'd been through, this was a woman of strength. I wouldn't have bothered if I wasn't attracted.

I could tell she would like me being in control, and I was right. I was aroused at removing, carefully, each piece of her clothing. She didn't go in for that ridiculous dress-up stuff. They were real, her undergarments; I am a woman, and I don't need to do anything special for you to understand that, her bra and panties said. And she was a woman, in the truest sense. When she was naked, I didn't think I could wait another second, but I made myself as I laid her down on the sofa and finally resumed the kiss I'd begun at the bar. It was incredible, the feeling of now allowing her to continue, giving the permission I'd held back all that time. And she was into it. Turned on, trembling and tensing. But there was something else, a kind of fascination, a surprise at it all. She probably hadn't had sex in years. There was no false show in her action, no playing out a role.

I had memorized the pages on her dresser, and I referred to them now. But not too close, not exactly; just enough to make her think, "Has it worked? Have I forced fate to instigate real events through the fiction I've written?"

"We shouldn't, Erin, doll," I whispered into the bone of her cheek. You could say I was playing a role, but it didn't feel that way.

That did it. She grabbed my head, pulled me to her, kissed like she knew magic was happening. And it did feel like magic— all the layers of history, tension, meaning, feeling, coming together in a perfectly paced crescendo—these perspectives I'd never considered before. I whispered not in her ear, but like the way she'd described in her prose, into her skin, "I don't think we should." Even I could feel how powerful the effect.

After, she was beautiful, lying there with her arm draped over her head, my mother's knitted blanket barely covering her chest. I'd orchestrated everything perfectly. Too perfectly. Perhaps I should change tack, I thought. Despite everything, I was fond of her. That day I watched her tapping at her notebook computer, her eyes focused somewhere deep inside, I knew I had to get to that place she'd reached, see it for myself.

And so I left her wanting. I could have made the sex last longer, but I didn't. She'd see the possibilities and want more.

That was better. I could feel her shaking when I entered her, and I almost came right then, but I knew how to stop myself— thinking of cleaning up the horse shit and that. I watched her when she closed her eyes. She was lovely. I felt for her with all her losses—the girl. I remember that day. It was terrible, all the sirens and the military guys everywhere. They thought it was terrorism at first, of course. I'd sat on my rickety, newly scraped porch, with my hunting rifle. I would protect our army families if I had to. I knew what they sacrificed for us. A little fucking girl; savages is what they are. Only they weren't. It was we who were the savages—a girl sacrificed for a half-hour pizza delivery guarantee. Fuck. A fucking marketing drone! I'd seen that girl—one of those bikes with the handle shooting out the back so Mom could hold it while the girl thought she was in charge. So much thought for such a simple thing. That's the kind of mother she was. I don't want to think of it anymore now. Sure as hell, she doesn't either. I'd made the woman giggle. Better work than any rifle could do.

4

———

ERIN

I t was a Tuesday when I first thought Gav had cottoned on. Normally, he had cereal for breakfast, any old kind we had. But on Tuesday, he rifled through the containers I'd pulled out and asked, "Don't you ever want anything else? Must get sick of the same thing over and over."

I was on edge all day. Surprisingly, this did not affect my writing. When I sat down, my mind wandered for ninety seconds or so, but I soon solidified the character Erika based on a study I'd read about many years ago. I couldn't even remember where I'd seen it, but the gist of the investigation was a character profile for creative people, which showed common traits, including these that stand out in my memory: self-confidence, attraction to complexity, and risk-taking. I had Erika stumble upon the study and find inspiration in this sketch of herself, as a writer, and before I knew it, the study thread had overlapped with the write-into-action experiment thread, and things got interesting. Here, we found legitimacy—to a degree our imaginations could accept—in the route Erika had taken in this half decade after her daughter's death. And then she went one step further: she had to raise the stakes. I could tell from the way the writing was going, in order to take the story to the next level. But what could she do? I had her ask the question herself, while she drove distractedly up a windy road at the edge of town. All of a sudden the sun lowered to a blinding angle that blanked out the world. That was what she needed, something bigger than sex, something as powerful as what had happened to Olivia, to achieve some more lasting satisfaction. The answer came to her first, instinctively, but she batted it away. She was not capable of murder. Erika tried to gather other ideas—ask Mick to do something dangerous, arrange a meeting in which Gav and Mick would run into each other, risk going to a military hangout with him. But none had the stickiness of the first one. No. Again her mind tickled at the aesthetic beauty of the symmetry. A full circle—death, rebirth, death again. Simultaneously, the rush of the muse took over—shards of detail piled up in just the perfect formation: he lived alone, the act could easily be written off as a building accident. She couldn't. Could she?

5

IRENE

The first thing I'll say is this: Gav loved me. I'm not saying he didn't love her, too, because I believe he did. It's just that in their case, there are some things you can't go back from. It started when he came into the BWS Liquors. We'd just had a flat screen installed to play ads and sport, but the girls and I turned it to *MKR* because I was right into it. Why shouldn't ordinary people get a chance at showing the world they're just as good as Famous So-and-So with an ass so big she should be hiding it, not wearing shiny Lycra to put it on display? We had opinions about *MKR*'s cast; we didn't like those city girls—the one with the crazy hair and the other one; we liked the ones from Mount Isa. Good country ladies who cared about family and roots.

He came in wanting a chilled bottle of a specific Sav Blanc—not the under-$15 bottles either. I went in back to see if I could find it in the chiller, and I did, and when I turned around, he was in there with me. He must have thought I meant for him to follow, and when he saw my surprise, we both laughed at the misunderstanding, as he clearly wasn't creepy. That was when I noticed his eyes. They were blue like lots of people's around here, but they weren't anything special—not extra bright or deep or brilliant. It wasn't the color that struck me, it was the effect—like they were closed. Sure, they were open in the sense that he wasn't asleep, but they didn't say, *have a chat with me*, or *I'm a happy person*, or even, *I'm an angry person*. They said nothing and forbade you from looking any further.

After the laugh, I looked away, like I imagined most people did. But I couldn't help myself from turning back. Surely there was some giveaway. I was a people person, that was what everyone said about me, and I didn't like this impenetrable quality.

I think that was what surprised him, because normally, people must see that look and say, all right, not trying that again. But not me. He looked right at me, with that Teflon gaze (unique words that produce an exact image in the mind, *metaphors*, he once explained, are the keys to articulation; where had he learned this?), like a dare, it seemed to me. I dare you to say something. But what? That was where I was stuck.

"Here it is," I said, holding up the bottle, as if it wasn't obvious from the label.

"There it is," he said, and led us back to the storefront. I watched his walk, and it struck me as strong. Not that he was flexing his arms and pushing his chest out like a bodybuilder. It had more to do with a heft—not fat or bulky—but solid, something you'd hold onto in a storm. But there was an angle to his posture that said, this is a secret about me. By the time we made it to the register, I knew I would have to find out what that secret was. Yes, man in fatigues, yes, I accept your dare.

6

ERIN

There was one little detail that kept niggling at the back of Erika's mind, whingeing in the melodic way Oanna used to do as she soothed herself to sleep, reminding me, I'm still here, don't forget about me. *It was that woman I'd seen the first night I'd spent at the pub with Mick. Surely, she wasn't paying much attention to me; if she did recognize me, it was probably in the same vague way I was trying to place her. But. If there were a murder investigation, she might remember Erika, and consequentially me, with Rick/Mick, and it wouldn't be difficult to put it together from there. I couldn't believe how quickly words like* murder investigation *had normalized themselves in my brain, swimming around with* get milk *and* where are the car keys? *It had taken time, but the unreality had transformed to taboo, a dirty secret, and then bravado, and finally, exhilaration and suspense: Would I? And so I made it my mission to work out who she was. This, I thought, was important to working out how to deal with the complication.*

Erika parked across from the pub, on the ocean side, and watched for her. If she came, it wouldn't be difficult to spot her. She had that pale pinky-blonde hair that was striking, and she wore hers long. So she looked out for that. As Erika did so, she tried to place where she'd seen her, but nothing shook loose. The sun was setting, and it struck her again, this idea of beauty being so close, but incapable of penetrating. Erika forced herself to look away from the spreading orange glow on the water, the liquid shape of the wind on its surface. Its beauty felt like Oanna dying again every time she looked.

The next day, when I looked over that bit, two things struck me. One, a tiny, but unsettling detail: I didn't like Oanna for the daughter character; I changed it to Olena. Two, Erika can look at the effect the sun's exit makes; she *should* look. And she should be able to let beauty penetrate. She should find a way. It felt vital, if she was going to these extremes, that she should.

And so, that next evening, at dusk, I rewrote: when Erika went to the pub to look for the girl with the pinky-blonde hair, she couldn't help but catch a peripheral view of the out-of-sight sun's setting rays, as they drenched the water's surface in color. Before she knew it she'd been watching for five minutes. Something akin to calm settled over her. She felt it mostly in her limbs, which had relaxed, dropped, nearly liquid as the ocean, and it was the most comfortable she'd been in a long while. She could feel the knots and pressure releasing in her shoulder and ankle joints. She turned away. For three days, Erika did this, at different times, in hopes of catching the girl.

When I later followed in Erika's footsteps, a similar feeling came over me on my third try, after I too had located the pinky-blonde girl and took a minute to see the sun lowering itself over the water. But after a minute, I snapped abruptly out of relaxation. No, I told myself. This was merely the power of suggestion. I had not found pleasure in this sunset, this death reminder, this memento mori. I looked away and made my posture rigid again. Some things should not be changed.

But I'd found her. She was walking in, the way she had for

Erika. She wasn't wearing exactly the same thing—her boots were different, more beat up; there was a gash in the toe I could see from there—and her T-shirt had a triangular logo I couldn't make out, rather than a retro rock band name.

At the bar, she was familiar with the girl who poured her drink. Were they friends the way Erika's version predicted? The sex of the bartender had been different, but so far, everything else more or less matched. Erika had been bold enough to approach her, but would I? My chest tingled at the idea. I didn't want to make a spectacle, especially in front of someone this girl knew, but wasn't this the quickest way to work out where I knew her from? I didn't want to come here every night. Gav would start to get suspicious, and if I did that, regular stroller walkers and joggers along the Strand would start to recognize me. On the other hand, just because I'd spoken to a friendly stranger at a bar, I wouldn't necessarily be considered suspicious. Probably no one would remember.

I was surprisingly calm as I made my way over the zebra crossing to the open-air bar front. I'd have to change that for Erika, who'd had to hold her hand in a pocket to conceal the trembling. When you're committed and the moment arrives, it feels almost fated. Since this is deeply akin to the feeling I experience when shards of a story begin to fall into place, I was more assured than ever I was on the right track. I had read about the neurobiological processes at work when a novelist creates, and I had come to think of us as more evolved, or at least more practiced, than the rest of the population in this vein; the sensation served as a reassurance of this theory.

As Erika's and my paths merged to approach the pinky-blonde girl, there was a religiosity to the transcendence I felt. I was getting somewhere, or maybe I was already there.

She looked at me as I meandered through a few hi-top tables, perhaps trying to work me out—my tailored slacks and matching top, my discreetly expensive tortoiseshell sunnies. She wasn't afraid to let her eyes travel my height. In fact, when she reached my eyes, she held my gaze. It was there; I was certain of it. She knew me.

"A Sav Blanc," I said. The bartender acknowledged me with a nod, and went back to her conversation with Pinky-Blonde, who was a head taller than me. Pinky-Blonde tried now to disguise her watching, but I could feel her, beneath her head scratch, or arm stretch. She was memorizing me.

The barkeep unscrewed the cap, inspected the wine glass, and poured. "Do you think he'll come to the shop tonight?"

I felt a frisson. What shop?

From the corner of my eye, I could see the pinky-blonde girl try to convey a message with a steely focus of her eyes. The bartender immediately understood she should change tack. She wasn't subtle.

"You know how you're always seeing your *neighbor* at that, um, coffee shop, and he's always annoying you about your lawn needing a mow? Didn't you say that last time I saw you?"

Pinky-Blonde's look said, *you're a freaking moron.*

The bartender returned with a silent, *I'm sorry.*

The giveaway: they both turned to me—as if they couldn't help it—at the same time. I smiled politely, what I hoped was benignly. Had they already known I was up to something? She must have recognized me on that previous night. I'd been correct to be concerned. But how to tease out any further connection without looking guilty?

It came to me instinctively, the solution. I was always excellent at chit-chat. People called me *charming*. "I hate when people see you trying to relax and pick that moment to chat you up," I said. "I have a gardener who always comes to talk to me just as I'm bringing my rubbish out in my nightgown. He has no sense of space."

35

"I like the way you put that," Pinky-Blonde said. "A sense of space."

She seemed to mean it, but I couldn't be sure; there was the fact of me barging in on *their* private conversation she could have been mocking.

"Doesn't exist in a bar," said the bartender, *Aggie*, according to her unevenly typed nametag.

"I saw you in here the other night. With that guy who's always sitting alone," Pinky-Blonde said, as if to emphasize the point.

"Yes, well." Keep your cards close to the vest. Never do exhibitionists gain respect.

"Is he nice? He's kind of good-looking, isn't he?"

"Mmm-hmmm," I said, noncommittally.

Getting nothing from me, they turned back to each other. The bartender spoke too loudly about someone she clearly hated. *Bitch. Slag.* It was as if she got something out of my hearing her say the words. Powerlessness has its manifestations. On the contrary, master of all the information, *I* felt incredibly powerful, though concerned about what Pinky-Blonde might do with her knowledge.

7

_____

IRENE

He came back, and it was like he wanted *me* to ask what he was coming here for, like there was some kind of line he needed me to cross in order for anything to happen. It was always the same day of the week. From the second that day was over, I waited for the next time. The weeks were long, but exquisitely so (I looked in the thesaurus for that word; the feeling was so strong that *special* wouldn't do it, and I thought he would like that—me finding the right word, as he spoke so perfectly, or *articulately*, as the thesaurus suggested).

He stayed precisely fifteen minutes each time, as if there were some threshold he'd cross if he were there any longer. The first time he returned, I was there with Celicia, who has a thing about being gruff to men. There was the usual kitchen chaos on *MKR*.

"Oh no he didn't," Celicia said of Gianni, who'd lost his cool at his fiancée for the third time in five minutes.

"He probably didn't say all that together. It's just the way they edit it," I said.

"Well, whatever. Still."

The door chimed, and there he was. Gavan Andrews, his credit card had said. Since his visit, each time I'd run my finger over the raised type of a card, I'd felt the same rush. This was new to me; normally, I went through the motions with men, who generally struck me as self-centered, thoughtless, and arrogant.

Now I watched as he purposely—or so it felt—avoided looking at me and made his way down the reds aisle. I could see him on the security camera beneath the counter. Under the grained, stop motion areal lens, he still had that posture. You couldn't walk past this man without turning around, and yet he conducted himself as if this couldn't be further from the truth. Like he was anybody. He picked up a bottle and inspected it, then another. That one he held, loosely, his thumb and fingers around its neck. The bottle pushed creases into his pant leg. I shivered now, around the corner, following him. I realized I'd been engrossed watching his grip on the bottle, the way it grazed his leg.

"Can I help you with something?" I asked. His gaze had settled on the second-highest priced Shiraz.

"Maybe."

"I've tried that one. It's lovely. Like Christmas."

"Like Christmas. Now that's a simile that could sell some red wine."

"Okay." My mother said that about everything. I never knew it was lovely. Mostly, she used it sarcastically. *Oh, look who decided to show up. How lovely, like Christmas.*

He was quiet, and I watched him shift that bottle to the crook of the same arm whose fingers dangled the first one, and then pick up another bottle in his other hand. I'd stood there too long and should have moved, but it didn't feel like he wanted me to. I was just starting to feel stupid when he spoke again.

"Tried this one? Like Australia Day?"

"Nah, that'd be Four X."

He smiled without looking at me; a shape-shifting one that transformed his face and then centimeter by centimeter disappeared.

"We had the rep from that vineyard here a while back. Bit of a wanker."

He laughed and put that one back on the shelf.

I smiled. But then I caught sight of his wedding ring. Why did it bother me so? He could have been my father. I didn't care if he was married; good on him.

"So which do you recommend?"

I should have kept my trap shut; for all the anecdotal information I gave out to customers, I didn't know much about wines. I didn't really like them as much as sparkling cider. I enjoyed the warmth of a red, the way it spread to my belly, but I couldn't tell why one was better than another—except for the really cheap ones that tasted sour. Normally, I pushed the one that was on special, but I could tell he'd be onto that. I picked the most expensive one.

"Oh, really? Why?"

I didn't want to lie; it seemed pointless. "It'll make my sales look good."

"Then this one it is."

He walked right to the register, and though I kept watching his eyes, Gavan didn't look me straight on again before he left.

I couldn't stop thinking about him. I rolled our exchanges around in my mind until they were smooth and familiar in my memory—polished and at a fingertip's blind reach.

8

ERIN

I didn't get much out of my conversation with Pinky-Blonde and Aggie. They wanted to be taken seriously, to be seen as mature. They pretended to know about topics that would help them to appear so: staying out late, drinking too much, knowing people. Mostly, they spoke to each other, with an effort to cast me as their audience, pulling faces and catching my eye for a reaction. They were nice-enough, naïve girls. But it was clear they needed role models. Aggie let slip that Pinky-Blonde worked in the Hermit Park shopping plaza. After I drank my wine, I excused myself, happy with this information.

It was the parking sticker that gave Pinky-Blonde away. "BWS Hermit Park" it said on an old Honda with a pair of pink fuzzy dice slung over the rearview. Erika and I would go and check. But then what? What would I do with this information? I held off going until the reasons revealed themselves.

The next day, I woke again thinking of memento mori; as if in this idea, in the image of not a sunset, but the idea of an off-stage sunset, and its manifestation in this part of the world, there was a clue to the way the story should go. *Remember, we must die.* Was there another, more vital way to look at things that I could live with? I turned to the Internet and typed in "memento mori." There was something taboo and heart-racing about the premise. Immediately, I was brought to an image page, full of photos of dead people—old women, beautiful young women, children in Victorian lace, splayed out with their doughy limbs. No one should have a page like this, was my first thought. My chest churned, my breath held, but I couldn't bring myself to look away. I clicked again and again, staring into their dead faces, looking for something that would guide me. But what I felt most was separate—separate from these people. They were somewhere else, some*thing* else.

Again, the fateful feeling: I was meant to come to this point; my mind was driving me toward it in a way the conscious me couldn't understand. Might I dare to think that this seemingly arbitrary literary tangent might be an extension of the mother-daughter connection no one can ever seem to locate the edges of? I remembered my leaking breasts when Olivia cried, the feel of my shirt dampening, sticking to my skin. The sensation now was so similar, I could feel relief sweeping over me, like I was getting closer.

This was where inspiration took hold.

I had Erika drive to the BWS. She didn't have to sit long until she saw Pinky-Blonde. This felt too easy to be perceived as mere coincidence by Pinky-Blonde. If she went in, clearly Pinky-Blonde would recognize her from the bar. What then? It wouldn't be odd for a local to pop up again in that way, but so many times in so few days? A conversation would doubtless ensue, and Erika would have to be prepared with whatever story she was going to tell of herself. She'd thought it through over and over, but kept getting stuck at the same point. Here's where it began: I noticed you at the Royal Hotel before we talked the other day, the night I was there on a first date. I noticed you knew the bartender. I'm so glad I saw you here because I wanted to ask you if you went to that bar often; he said he did, and if you'd seen him there before, I wondered whether you thought there wasn't something a little strange about that guy.

But what? What would be strange enough to raise the kind of after-the-fact suspicion that wouldn't be so obvious that it seemed like a cover-up? She knew the power of suggestion. If she put the idea in Pinky-Blonde's head, chances are, she'd start looking at him suspiciously—especially after something happened. But if it was clumsy, it would later be—*aha!*—easy to work out Erika's guilt. So? What could plausibly concern her?

I wrote around for a few minutes, but nothing came. I looked over Rick's character questionnaire, and couldn't remember which of the traits were true and which I'd fictionalized. Or perhaps, more accurately, I *could* remember, but chose to blur the lines; the truth didn't feel important. I liked the effect of the final product better than an accurate version could have turned out. So much so that I decided I would switch over to his real name; *Rick* was starting to jar, seem superfluous, arbitrary.

Yes, all the details were in place, but I couldn't decide ahead of time where things should go; everything I tried felt artificial. I'd have to pants it. The familiar thrill set in. I was as keyed up to see what might happen as any reader might be—probably more.

Erika parked halfway across the mostly empty line of parks, as if that was the place she normally chose. She straightened her lipstick before leaving the car, not so much to look better, but to look *right*, the way she imagined she should look doing this. Red lips were important. Not everyone could wear them, and she could, and that would say something. Nothing you could put your finger on, but an intangible that mattered. She pressed her lips together and smudged her fingers toward the edges.

Sunglasses cocked on her nose, she cradled her purse like a baby in one arm. Nonchalance was probably oozing off her.

This is where the action on the page shriveled and died, but that heart-racing, toe-tapping bliss remained. I walked around the perimeter of our garden for a few minutes: took in the blowy surface of the ocean, focused on a few sailboats over by Maggie Island, thought I saw a turtle. And then I sat back down to the computer; a crow cawed. I closed my eyes, the brightness of the sky captured beneath my lids in color bursts, and when I pictured these characters at BWS, what I saw was that ridiculous bottle of wine Gav had brought home the other night. I didn't know why it should bother me that he wanted pleasure, too. And what could be simpler to enjoy than a good wine? Of course we weren't going to talk about this kind of motivation while we drank the wine, and if I did ask, he'd deny it—say it was the first one he saw or some such bullshit.

Again, I was stuck. I tried to imagine Pinky Blonde at the counter, and I was just getting a good look at her, seeing the reflection of the sunlight on her glossy hair, when I realized exactly where the inspiration had been headed. I needed to switch gears: What if I experienced *first*, and *then* put the experience into my writing after the fact? How might that affect the writing? What would this change in the work accomplish? Would it make the work not fiction anymore, but something else? Something closer to whatever I was trying to achieve? But what about the responsibility element? Was I trying to avoid that? No. No, that wasn't it. I knew for sure because again, I had that feeling: *closer*. I knew about guilt, that Zen view of it, that soldier's view of it: guilt was a pointless emotion that clouded rationality and what needed to be done. People who worried about the possibility of guilt could not achieve the most important—always the most complex—tasks. Because at that level, everyone shared the guilt; nothing was so black and white as to be free of it. I imagined myself finally beyond it and now onto the more crucial, truer, and more valuable level of the experiment. Yes. This was right in every sense.

I nearly ran out of the house and drove, shaky, keyed up, in order to find out what the change in order would stir up. As I drove, thoughts raced through my head. I knew the risks of "reporting" on your life in fiction writing: endless pages of boring, meandering crap that broke all the rules of fiction craft —making for a wonky, self-indulgent story that pleased no one but the writer. But this wouldn't be that. It would be research, *creation*, only played out in reality. It wasn't my existing life I was trying to capture in fiction. It was an extension of the art, something no one had done before, and it was exciting as fuck. I felt like I could do anything. Even reach my dead daughter? I wouldn't let myself be so concrete. But.

I slowed my breathing along with my pace as I made my way to the door. Pinky-Blonde looked over from the television immediately as the door opened, as if she'd trained herself to, not, I suspected, because she wanted to. She made eye contact and nodded her head before realizing who I was, which registered with more of a start than I would have liked.

I resisted the urge to swallow.

"The woman from the bar; I'd love to chat to you, but I wouldn't want to invade your personal space." She smiled, looking for approval of either her remembrance or clever usage. Maybe she *was* just innocently surprised to see me.

"And you're . . . *Irene*." Her nametag was pristine, as if she polished it regularly. And her presence seemed to ask, why wouldn't she? I had been mistaken earlier; she *did* seem to take pride in what she did. Her counter was sensibly arranged, dust-free. "What can I help you with?"

"Hmmmm. Not quite sure. Thought I might try something new." Yes, that was good. It would get her talking.

"Any special occasion?"

"Well, it's a little embarrassing, but that man you saw me with, that was our first date." I brought my hand to cover half my face. I saw it as Erika's hand, as a gesture she might make.

Irene swallowed as if this idea made her uncomfortable, but she tried to cover it up with a polite smile. "Why would that be embarrassing?"

"Well, to be honest, I really like him." As Erika, I darted my eyes up and down playfully; I was getting into the role. It was quite fun, exploring this character.

"That's wonderful."

"I hope so." I had Erika draw breath, as if something were weighing on her. Almost instantly, as if everything had been pointing me in exactly this direction, I relaxed seamlessly into Erika's skin; after so much writing time, I knew her, her gestures came naturally—and there wasn't the self-consciousness my own had these days. It wasn't as if I were acting as Erika, but at that moment, I was Erika, and Erika was me.

"What is it?" Irene was friendly, warm. She had an inviting way about her, as if she could metaphorically use wine to connect with people on any level, but not on purpose, not with guile. Even if Erika wasn't playing toward it, I could see how someone might open up to Irene. In fact, I felt I wanted to—but I was getting confused; which bits of motivation were mine, and which were the character's? In another flash, it came to me —I had to abandon myself completely. From this moment forward, in every interaction with another human being, I would be Erika. "Erin" would only be the figure at her computer, writing. Again, that fated feeling that I'd uncovered

The Way Things Should Be flashed over me. I made a vow: I was now Erika.

Shaking her head, this Erika brought herself back to the moment; there was Irene's question to answer. In another scenario, they could be close; Erika could see herself feeling proud of this girl, maternal toward her youthful confidence and openness. "Well, I can't help but feel like there's something he's holding back."

"Like what?"

Erika shrugged, shook her head. "Wait a minute."

Irene inclined her head.

"You were at that bar. Do you go there often?"

The girl blinked twice, like Erika had slapped her. Shit! What if she'd seen Erika watching her from outside the bar? She thought she'd been careful, but how could she be sure? Now that she'd merged the roles, the tension was incredible. Everything—not just a storyline—was truly at stake.

"I guess so. I'm friends with that bartender."

"So, can I ask you this without sounding suspicious?" Oh! Why had she used that word? The word *suspicion* would only plant suspicion. It occurred to her that Erin would have avoided that trap; already, she was *becoming* Erika.

"Sure. What is it?"

She fumbled, trying to put on a front for some reason. Oh, this was trouble—good for the book, bad for the reality. If you know what's good for you, run, Erika, run. And yet, she stayed.

"Like I said, I feel there's a secret he's holding back from me . . ."

"Like what kind of secret?"

"Like a girlfriend, or a wife." That was good, perfect actually, but Irene had gone white. Did Erika look too suspicious now to pull off lies? Erika needed to get out of here; surely that was panic in Irene's face. But wait. Did that mean that perhaps there *was* a wife or girlfriend? Did she care if there were?

"So, have you seen him there with anyone else?"

"Um. Not that, um, I can recall. I think he's a builder or something. Seen him there with some guys in yellow shirts—after the time when they're not supposed to be wearing that."

We both looked away, but then caught each other retreating to eye level simultaneously. "I guess that doesn't sound too suspicious. Perhaps I'm being paranoid." Or, perhaps Irene had more to do with Mick than she was letting on?

"Perhaps." Irene swallowed. What was she hiding? Had Erika walked into some complicated situation she couldn't begin to comprehend? Had she overestimated her monopoly on knowledge? Did anyone ever come into this shop? She needed a break from this stare-down and an excuse to get out of here without looking even guiltier by bolting.

"What about some wine?" Erika said. "That's what I'm here for." Surely the quick change was even more suspicious.

"Right." Irene walked straight to the reds without showing her cards. "How about this bottle?" Now everything she said seemed to have subtext to Erika.

So was it truly bizarre that this was exactly the bottle Gav had brought home the other night, or was this further evidence that she was being paranoid? Irene's look was a poor copy of the kind of look Gav had taken on since Livvie's death. *You don't see what you think you see, and if you do, I'll fucking kill you if you bring it up; and yet, somehow, I'm still a nice, likeable person.* Hers got the likeable part down, but merely flirted with caginess; if you just asked twice, she'd tell you whatever you wanted, but wished it might be otherwise.

Maybe Erika *was* just being neurotic. Surely the staff were told to promote certain wines, and besides, it was a smallish store with a smallish selection, so this was probably her go-to suggestion. And though it was on Gav's way home from work, and so the obvious place to stop, the coincidence sat funny with Erika. So funny that she took the recommended wine and left, quickly, fumbling, twice dropping her keys on the way to the car. The two of them were probably keeping the shop in business.

9

GAVAN

The first time, he told her to meet him on a Monday, at the dog beach, at Pallaranda. He'd never run into anyone there. The dog was Olivia's, and Erin barely looked at it. Gav had to take over feeding him when he uncovered the dry-food bucket, one day when Erin was sleeping in, and saw it was empty. He noticed the dog looked like hell and probably hadn't been walked or fed in a while. Another casualty.

It was a nice thing, taking the dog, walking at sunrise, and after dark when he got home. Bud was a good dog, a golden retriever, nothing fancy, and he slept outside Olivia's door every night, and most days. He looked sorry when Gavan held the lead up for him, as if he didn't want to be a bother, knew he reminded us all of The Firecracker.

On the desolate beach, they'd started out bullshitting about wines, but the conversation had quickly turned to more intimate territory without him realizing, like she'd charmed him with wine speak, and out came all these feelings he didn't even know he had. Then there was an awkward silence after he caught himself about to mention something about Erin, during which all he could think was how young Irene was. She moved a hair closer to him, and he could feel her inviting warmth, and she laughed at herself and said, "I'm sorry; I do that to people. I don't mean it, but it happens. They tell me things."

"That's a gift, you know."

"Right. Well. While we're telling, I should probably tell you that I Googled you."

It was a loaded confession; it meant she knew everything, and his first instinct was to call the dog back from the swim he was enjoying, and excuse himself. But she voiced these exact thoughts, and this put him so far out of his comfort zone that he was dumbstruck. People were generally afraid to talk to him about anything, much less about his dead daughter and recluse wife.

Without realizing, they'd stopped walking, and he turned to her right there and kissed her. He hadn't known he was going to do it. He couldn't believe how natural it felt. Easy, nice. Comforting. And hot. Because it was the wrong thing to do. Everything else he did because it was the right thing to do. This was liberating in its complete disregard for his sensibilities. It was all for him. Fuck, it felt good. He grabbed her ass, and he felt her push into him. When she moaned, he wanted to rip her jeans off right there. But no. He could wait. Or not.

He yanked himself away. Her breath shuddered in his face, and he almost went back in. He looked at Bud, swimming, and then thought, eh, leave him. Let him enjoy the waves. He gave the whistle call to stay and took Irene's hand, leading her back up to the heavy scrub. He knew about snakes and spiders, but that was part of it: if he died, so be it. He felt duty-bound to Erin, but he had started to feel like she would be better without him, that his presence was too painful. Hers certainly was. If some deadly thing went for Irene, well, he had a soldier's instincts. She'd be fine.

She had protection, which was a good thing, because he wasn't ever going to have a kid again. That was for certain. She was young, but wasn't dazzled by the romance of it, which made him slightly self-conscious, as if she might be less interested than him. And so he worked harder to impress her, to turn her on. At the very end, he caught her looking closely at him and thought there must be something in that look. It was enough to bring him over the edge. When he collapsed onto her, she put her arms around him. He hadn't expected it, but he knew from his reaction that there was no turning back now.

10

————

ERIN ~~ERIN~~ ERIKA

W hen you get past a certain distance from normalcy, there are things you find out about yourself that are horrific. Because of the way it propelled the story, even these fascinated Erika, in an incredibly satisfying way. It was all working—better than any story she'd told before. Made her wonder if the greats had been onto this method. More, deeper; she was so alive, she couldn't believe she was the same person she'd been after the child had gone; of course she wasn't.

The ironic thing was, she was *living*. It almost had nothing to do with Mick; she had been right about that—with the right caressing of the plot, she could have used anyone in that role. That was the trick, getting the characterization right (whatever it might be) so that the actions took on a propulsion that the readers almost couldn't bear. That was what made them stay up all night. And she'd worked Mick out, hadn't she? That was why it was all spinning so quickly out of control.

It was a Monday when she worked out Mick had been

spying on her. First she saw his truck pull away from the museum parking lot—right next to her house—and then when she got home, there was a muddy boot print on the carpet. She stared at it, knowing it was not Gav's. She'd know his boot print anywhere, but that was moot: he'd never leave a mess. He wasn't that sort of person.

Her mind flashed to Mick's truck, and immediately she made the connections. She hadn't been making things happen —maybe at first there were a few coincidences, or even more: the power of her intention had set things in motion. She wouldn't be the first to accomplish that. But, what she'd mistaken for her "power" was nothing more than Mick's deceit. She felt defiled. She'd been doing something pure, something that had made her feel closer to Olivia, that had made her feel alive, and he'd been fucking with her all this time. There was no reason to kill him; there was no test of her "powers."

Erika should have been relieved. She didn't really want to kill anyone and had been catching herself testing her sanity with the way she handled everyday encounters, but what she was left with as her heart slowed down was disappointment. Was she a killer? *Did* she want to kill someone? Had it been about that all along? If so, what was her motivation? Was she so warped as to think this would bring about some justice in the world? One random death in exchange for another? She wanted to say no, that's ridiculous, but in this moment of pondering, Erika looked up and caught sight of one of the memento mori photos she'd printed out: a little girl and her mother—both in their final sleep, in matching high-necked lace. She was nearly there, close to Olivia somehow. She could feel it. Serenity.

So it wouldn't come about in the way she had originally thought, but that was okay. She was ready to risk everything. She had nothing left anyway. She realized that was what this had always been about—how far would she go to get out of this stage, to get somewhere new, start something new, whatever it was? It wasn't as simple as wanting to laugh, as she'd originally thought. It was a clean break she was after. Leaving behind who she was for someone new.

At first she was suspicious of why he'd left the boot print. Surely, he had been very careful up to that point for her not to have realized he'd been breaking in and reading her manuscript. Why be messy now? Erika's chest went cold; did he *want* her to know he'd been reading the pages?

She tried to work through the possibilities. Her computer was where she did her best thinking—pulling the strings together into something coherent. If he read the pages and knew her plan to kill him, then he was fighting back in some way here. But how? The thrill coursed through her blood. See? This was why pantsing was the best writing method. She never could have foreseen this complication if she'd planned out a plot from the outset. If he's also creating the story, she thought, this is a deeper complication. It's like performance art, or Shakespeare in the Park, where the lines between actor and audience are confused. He's taking part. He's deepening the story's entrenchment in reality.

And the fact that she *was* Erika, rather than just writing about some character named Erika, gave it infinitely more oomph. This would be her swan song. It was almost unbelievably perfect. Even she didn't know what would happen when she met him on the night in question. Would she get the chance to see if she had what it took to kill him, or was he going to beat her to the punch? Her hand was shaking from excitement. She got up and poured herself a glass of that expensive red. God, it was good.

Okay, wait. Another think about Mick's snooping. Could he have had a benevolent motivation? Did he want her to write about it to help her in some way? *Think.* Reading the pages, he would know *Erika's* thoughts, allow her to think *she* had the power. *Could* it be a kindness? A thoughtful indulgence to go along with her harebrained scheme, under the assumption it would come to nothing? How could a woman like her murder him?

Surely no one was so kind as to help someone plot their own murder out of compassion. Still, Erika couldn't help but sense that Mick did have feelings for her, genuine feelings.

Then why leave a sloppy print now, after being so careful all this time? If Erika saw the print, became suspicious, wrote about it, and then he read her suspicions—what then? Nobody would know what was truth and what was intended as deceit. Everyone would be in the know, but no one would know anything for certain. It was a test of intuition, of guessing the outcome, seeing how good you were at working out mysteries.

The problem was, she didn't know Mick the way she knew fictional Mick. She didn't know his motivations, his desires, his agenda. And this meant she'd always be in the dark. All she could do was continue with her plan, try to get to know him better, so that she could predict his moves as best she could, and see where the chips fell.

She was not as devastated as one might think. In fiction writing, this happens all the time; you write along one avenue only to find that actually, that's not the way things are headed. There is another way in which the story is going, all by its own propulsion. It's exciting, addictive. And such doubling back is all part of the process. Especially when your characterization is incomplete. She'd have to make more plans before she tried anything, get to know him.

The other thing she had to do now was research. How to get away with murder? Normally, she would interview someone for authenticity and accuracy: a forensics expert, for example. But that wouldn't work here; she'd give herself away. And she couldn't check anything out of the library either, or it would be on her record. The bookshops in town were small; she'd never buy a forensics or crime book without being noticed. And she'd never written that sort of thing, so she didn't own any volumes on crime. A road trip: she'd have to drive to the closest big city where she'd be anonymous, pay for gas and any purchases in cash, try not to stick out to anyone, and then come back.

Erika couldn't sleep the night before her trip. She tossed all night, while Gavan slept intolerably soundly. But once she got out of bed in the morning, things had solidified in her mind. She was resolute. She was going to Brisbane, she was going to buy a book, and she was going to come home. It would be an overnight trip, but she would come up with an excuse.

Gavan came down as the coffee brewed, showered and fully dressed in fatigues. It had been a while since she'd really looked at him, and she got that sense again that there was something different about him.

"I'm staying overnight with Lottie at some holiday house she rented for the week. She said it's about an hour's drive from here." He didn't know Lottie, and for good reason. There *was* no Lottie. But they didn't question each other, because too many questions led to too many questions, which only led to one little girl they didn't want to think about.

"Right-o."

Did he look relieved? She couldn't blame him; Erika certainly exhaled greatly when he left in the mornings. He ate his toast standing outside over the waterfront, poor fucking man—see, already the thoughts sprinted there; this was why she never wanted to be around him. He compacted his cloth hat at the worn creases and slid it into his back pocket (she never could believe how soft those fatigues were, used to love to hug him in those, rub her face in the laundry-fresh softness), took a last draught of coffee, and kissed the air near her ear.

Even the drive to Brisbane was thrilling. The most boring stretch of road known to man, and Erika couldn't stop her heart from racing. "*Mummy*, you're being so *silly!*" Olena loved the opportunity to say that to her. How many times had she gotten it wrong—like when she was measuring out detergent for the laundry, or packing her lunch? But when she used it at the right occasion, well, you never saw a face light up so. "Did I get it right, Mummy? Did I?"

"You did, darling! Aren't you clever?"

"I am; I am." So serious, head nodding. A beautiful, shining girl. With a halo of light. How she could be so interested in everything she did—piling blocks in a bucket, mounding sand into a heap. Yes, Erika could watch her for hours. That is precisely how interested Erika felt in this present adventure. She wouldn't get it wrong. Olena was with her. She'd "reached" her substantially enough to actually hear her words. That much was clear.

Erika sang along to the old songs played on the ABC, noted the funny bumper stickers, remarked on the Jesus freaks. She was eighteen again, only better, cleverer and more comfortable in her skin, and not alone. She was definitely not alone. When she filled up the tank, she was careful not to make remarkable small talk; she kept to the general pleasantries. *You're so silly, Mummy!* She'd be one of dozens of middle-aged women in floral sundresses. She'd melt into the scenery. She wore no makeup. No expensive handbag. She could feel herself pixilate into obscurity.

There was a large-chain bookshop in the shopping centre in

the middle of town, and it opened at ten. She'd be there by eleven, hopefully find what she needed, and get out.

Amazingly, they had only one book on the topic; three copies. It was new, on the recommended non-fiction shelf. She picked it up with a very passable look of surprised interest, as if she wouldn't expect it to be so interesting, but that last episode of *Poirot* had got her thinking, and she happened to pick it up and found herself engrossed. Surely, if she logged onto Amazon, there would be hundreds, if not thousands of such titles. The back matter confirmed her beliefs: "armchair forensics," they called the growing category. Probably, even if someone did recall her purchase, it wouldn't be remarkable at all—she was one of a million would-be sleuths. Relief coursed through her. She let the best writer's feeling in the world sweep over her—she'd unwrapped her destiny; some mystical force had given her the power to make such a turn and then another in order to do so. Now the pull toward the conclusion was fierce. She looked down at her fingers on the pages and saw they were trembling, as if she couldn't get there fast enough.

The first words she underlined were, *Every contact leaves a trace.* It was poetic and simple, and yet a practical statement of the kind readers would lodge in their minds to whip out later when they were trying to work out a mystery. It put into words the concerns she'd had upon gathering information on forensics: she didn't want to make contact with people who might be able to trace the remarkable behaviors back to the crime. The next line she highlighted was: *The perpetrator of a crime will bring something into the crime scene and leave with something from it, and both can be used as evidence.* Genius: again, this info wasn't surprising, but seeing it in this way made her hyperaware of the care she needed to take with Mick. She was on the right track.

And then another line on the physical evidence found at a crime scenes: *Only human failure to find it, study and understand it, can diminish its value.*

The further she got into the material, the more poetic the trope of murder and forensics became. It was the DNA that stole the show, an entity so delicate, but fundamental to life; understand it, and you would control life itself. What goal was more central to literature? No wonder the armchair forensics titles were outselling cookbooks.

And then literature came into the picture; it was Sherlock Holmes who popularized and gave credence to forensics. The signs were everywhere.

Sherlock Holmes? At this point, she was struck by her heretofore cavalier attitude about *murder*. MURDER. Despite all the satisfying reassurance her work was providing, could she possibly kill someone? This was not Sherlock Holmes.

She made herself page through to the crime scene analyses. But it was all so distasteful: the body, identifying marks, gas collection in organs and tissue. Her own daughter would have been spoken about this way by someone.

Disposing a body in the ocean was too risky: it might rise up as gas collected in the tissue and cavity. They called this a "floater." Disgusting. Could a person become merely bait? How was this possible? What had she been thinking? Life was sacred. She'd never be able to go through with it. Would she? For her daughter, yes, she could. It was all she could do for her now, and she owed her that much.

The key was to prepare as best she could, then put herself in the situation and see what happened. That was the real test; she could only plan so far until circumstances took over.

She forced herself to continue reading the book. Perhaps she could just concentrate on the writing. If there was a connection between her writing and reality, then surely things would take care of themselves. She knew that in her bones. Her whole life was a testament to it. Her daughter had been sacrificed to it. She was overthinking. The thing to do was to jump right in. And so she put her head down and wrote.

Practicalities: from her reading, the only methods of murder (God, that word!) she could probably even manage were what forensics science called "blunt force trauma," which amounted to hitting him over the head with something, or poison (here she flashed to visions of fairy tales and Nazis). But poison was too risky—there was the procurement of the chemicals, which could be traced (thank you, terrorists), and the chance it wouldn't work. So, blunt force trauma. Surely there was something in his house she could hit him with. She remembered a pair of old stained glass lamps, which probably came with the house, and a few paint cans.

Erika wore her favorite silk slip beneath a simple cream dress she used to love. She'd worn it when Gav was handed over the brigade flag, and when he'd received a plaque from the governor general. It had been years since the icy feel of it on her skin, the satisfying pluck of straightening the spaghetti straps. A thing of beauty, but merely another thing whose beauty would be folded away in a drawer, leaving her life as ugly as it had been before her encounter with it.

She parked her car three blocks away and around the corner to avoid anyone recalling it by Mick's house. The sky was just darkening; evening seemed to take forever to get itself together up here. Something that would startle you in other parts of the world with its sudden cloak swung over everything was an enormous achievement here, a slow, painful birth, a death. When the process was finally completed, it was always with relief. There was the lasting image of this town's imposter sunset, though—reminding everyone what they so easily forgot every day—

remember, we must die. When you really understood that, the world was a very different place.

Once she started writing, the sunset image helped her to refocus on Olivia, because every word brought her closer in spirit to her daughter. "Silly Mummy! *Puleaze* can I have a choc-cy?" Suddenly, she could rally her thoughts around the murder as a necessary step. Erika must be brave to get to her daughter again. Was she strong enough to endure this distasteful act in pursuit of being somehow reunited with her daughter? *Memento mori.* She wanted some kind of tingly reaction to the words pouring from her, but that initial frisson of moments ago had left her as focus consumed her. Maybe she was just in a mood? Sometimes you didn't feel like writing, but you wrote anyway. Feelings weren't always to be trusted.

Still, her heart raced as the ballpoint bit into the page, the momentum—good or bad—tightening her muscles, her grip on the pen aggressive. The symbolism, the idea of some meaning to her actions gave a more palatable presentation of the action, even if it was more an in-general feeling than a specific logical thread. This was where art was better than life. You didn't have to be so black and white, to broadcast everything in sound bites.

Besides, she'd become knowledgeable in the subject area, and this always lent authenticity to the story. Even Erika herself was impressed with how convincing it all was: *The greater the surface area struck by the blow, the less the injury.* So, she'd have to keep her strike focused with a smaller object. If she was going to use the lamp, she'd have to turn it over and hit him with the narrow base. *It is difficult to determine what instrument caused a blunt-force injury.* The book went on to describe the types of wounds related to the victim trying to defend himself: on the palms and ulnar (little finger) side of his forearm. Abrasions, contusions, lacerations, and even broken bones could be defensive wounds. It was the wounds Mick might inflict on her that could get her into trouble. So, she would need to be careful to not receive any *contusions* (bruises). She'd need to wipe prints. Another thing to watch out for would be her saliva. They would be able to profile her from her saliva, so she would not be able to kiss him on the chance they could identify her "junk DNA." Even cleaning up might not remove all blood traces. It was too messy. At every turn, she would be undone. She didn't know where to go from here.

She shook out her hair, secured it up in an elastic, closed her eyes, and stretched her fingers before gripping the pen. Right.

Micko didn't answer the door on the first knock. There was no bell. Just a bare pair of wires twisted, poking out as if in wait. Erika could feel her breath becoming shallow and tried to settle it with a long inhale. Her fingers trembled. She knocked again, tried to peer into the leaded glass peephole. It was too wavy to see through.

Finally, footfalls down the stairs. She couldn't stop thinking about the boot print. What was his motivation here, at this moment? It was important she know this to get the upper hand.

When he opened the door, it was with a grand gesture. "Come in." Immediately, she smelled rosemary. Lamb. She hadn't expected lamb.

"Smells good."

He smiled. "Drink?"

Erika nodded and settled herself on the sofa, placing her handbag at the base of the stained glass lamp. He disappeared into the kitchen.

Fuck it. This was too slow. She needed more action. Tapped her pen on the notebook edge. Probably a reader would want sex now. The scene was set for it. Maybe sex could provide something unique. Funny, at the word, her mind settled on Gavan. He had always been excellent in that area, with his distance that people were always trying to bridge. He could have had sex with anyone, probably. It was childish, but the idea of this always turned her on.

Micko was different. There was a sense he really wanted her to want him. Strangely, this knitted them in a way she'd not experienced before. Beneath it all, wasn't this what everyone wanted? And so, now, playing this game, she had the sense they were playing at playing it. Beneath that: a kindness, a loveliness. Was this just the artist in her, or was it really there? She tested herself. Could she see herself lifting this lamp, and smashing him in the head with the narrow base? Kiss, kill. Where had she heard that before? She forced herself to picture it as he handed her a glass of Sav Blanc. Had he been playing with that beer-only offer at the bar that time? She made herself visualize the whacking over and over again, to desensitize herself. But she shuddered inwardly.

"You okay?"

And maybe outwardly.

"Yes, yes."

"You have a murderous look about you."

No, no. He wouldn't say that. But maybe he would. It would say let's not do this. *Kiss, kill?* Funny, she could see through a crack in the story an alternate ending: one where they live here in this house, and she helps him to brush varnish onto decking, and they get really into good sex. But there isn't the desire there like the one pushing her to reach Olena. She can't get there from here. *Mummy! I don't wanna go to the store!* Her little fists at Erika's thighs. Then that defiant pinch, which stung like hell. How she'd prided herself on the manner in which Olena would always apologize without being asked to. *Sorry for being naughty, Mummy.*

She didn't finish the scene. It didn't seem to matter anymore. Things had crescendoed. What happened on paper or at Micko's house was in motion, was gaining speed, rolling her down to some kind of ending. Yes, an ending. Her ending. Why hadn't she realized before? A deep sigh. Finally, she'd worked it out.

> You don't know how you got here
> You just know you want out
> —U2, "Hold Me, Thrill Me, Kiss Me, Kill Me"

It wasn't a song of theirs she'd particularly liked or even knew well, but now she listened to it. The meaning mirrored everything she was doing here, as if she'd tapped into some collective unconscious that was right on. She got up to go, this time leaving the pages out in the open on her desk. So what if Gavan saw them now? This was it. Tomorrow, what would be would be.

11

IRENE

I wanted to tell him about his wife's affair, but I knew it would ruin everything. Part of the appeal of us was that he had taken the initiative to do what he wanted; if he knew his wife was doing the same, where would the illicitness be? I understand about affairs. I see enough handsy couples springing for the pricey bottles on their way next door to the hotel. I don't feed off it the way Aggie does. In fact, it makes me feel sick, thinking of the deceitful ways people pleasure themselves. For me, knowing his wife was cheating made the whole thing easier for me. Besides, I liked her, and now I didn't feel so bad about fucking her husband. I was glad I'd done the Google search.

Sex had never been all that as far as I could tell. I think he saw that about me the first time, and he cared to have me enjoy, which was nice. That was when I really saw his kindness. He was good at it, too. Not practiced, but he had a natural way of being—that same impenetrable quality as when I'd first met him—that made you want to rip into him. I found it irresistible.

"What would you want with someone like that?" Aggie, my bartender friend, had asked. "There's no future, no availability, no commitment."

How could I explain that that was the appeal? I was me, but there was this other neat part that slotted in now, with him. I didn't need any more than that. Didn't want any more than that. I liked that he had another life that had nothing to do with me. It made the life we shared all the more special, because we couldn't have it all the time, couldn't waste it or take it for granted. When he expressed my own feelings back to me exactly, I felt relief, like everything had been perfectly worked out and I'd figured out life. What next? World peace? I really did feel I could do anything; I didn't know why people made this life thing so complicated. It didn't need to be.

"Metaphor," Gavan said, "is when you apply one word for an object to which it is not literally applicable."

Literally applicable. It sounded lovely, like something Cinderella's fairy godmother would sing as she magicked all her dreams into reality. I'd used the word, but only sort of knew its meaning.

"Like when your wine smells like Christmas, only instead of being 'like,' you set up the words so your idea replaces the original thing. A powerful act."

"Your cock is heaven."

"You're a natural." Oh, the giggles were a clear blue sky.

At home, I poured out Mom's tea, enjoyed knowing her one-sugar-plus-a-splash-of-milk habit. Dad was famous for making his own tea and even washing up without a trace, just so he didn't have to make one for anyone else. I enjoyed her complaining over the newspaper headlines as if they were a personal affront. *More legislation for those poor farmers. How is anyone expected to survive?* I doubted she knew what the legislation was about, but that wasn't the point. If anything, looking over her shoulder, her long, grey-tinged plait down to the bench, this familiar ritual seemed *more* pleasing to me in that it was mine alone. Nothing to do with my time with Gavan.

I wasn't even sure I'd considered this intimate knowledge of Mom as a benefit before, or even considered it at all, but all sorts of ordinary things began peeking out at me, demanding I recognize their charm. I'd never been happier.

But then it started nagging at me. The whole thing was built on the premise that Gavan's other life was the way he left it, too. Only it wasn't. His wife was with Mick, and from what she said, she had strong feelings for him. How could I not tell Gavan?

"You can't," Aggie said. "It's not right. Think about all the movies, when this kind of thing is eating somebody up, so they go and confront the person. And it's always a gigantic mistake. It ruins everything. He has a secret, and so does she. So what? For all you know, he already knows, and you're part of some sick game where he's holding all the cards."

I couldn't get that idea out of my head. It was ruining everything. For such a short time—perfection. And now this. I felt, more than anything, that I had to restore the equilibrium of the way we were.

But I knew Aggie was right about one thing. Telling him would only make things worse. And so I took it one day at a time, trying to keep it to myself.

And at first, I thought I'd gotten the hang of it. I Googled "keeping secrets" and followed the best advice I could find. I imagined the secret as a bird (or the secret is a bird, metaphorically, which if you think about it *is* powerful), watched the bird in my mind's eye as it flew out of sight, and told myself it was now gone forever. Initially, the active energy required to keep the thought at bay made me cranky; any additional issue—no matter how small, *"No, I cannot remember to buy the cheap kind of eggs on my way home!"*—took too much concentration when I

67

was still juggling the bird out of sight, and I began to snap at people. I became distracted, made mistakes on the till, dropped things. But as the days progressed, it got easier. The bird had become a benign midday shadow (too bad I couldn't share that gem with Gavan), and pretty soon I could ignore it altogether. I started to feel like myself again.

Until I made a really stupid mistake. I drove to the big house up at the point. I told myself I'd just do a loop on the road in front, from the museum up to the fort; I was determined to do just that, but then, after I'd turned around to head back, I noticed that guy Mick's truck. It was impossible to miss it; his construction company's logo was posted on the side: *ProBuild*. Made into one word like that, as if he was cleverer than everyone else who had to use two words to say such a thing. He was in the driver's seat, eating something wrapped in paper, and watching the house. I made a right at the end of the block and parked the car to get my thoughts in order. Yes, I had a sinister feeling about his presence there. Why would he be watching the house? Gavan or his wife could be in danger. What did anyone really know about this Mick character? I couldn't keep it to myself. What if something terrible happened and I could have prevented it? I did recon the following two days, and there he was. Watching, eating, like the house was there for his entertainment.

I went back and forth about this for a couple of days, alternately believing I was overreacting, needed to stop watching *COPS* and *NCIS*, and then believing that I could not keep my mouth shut. Maybe an anonymous call to the police was in order? Perhaps Mick was just so smitten he couldn't keep away. Still, even that was extreme behavior and could be headed somewhere bad. Or it could be love in its purest form. What did I know?

It was exhausting. More dropping things, messing up at

work. I didn't like the effect and wanted to straighten it out. I gave myself a deadline. Life is simple, I kept telling myself. If I couldn't think of a sticky reason not to by Friday, then I would tell Gavan about his wife's affair and Mick's house-watching. If that brought about the end of us, I'd deal with it. Simple. Child's play.

12

GAVAN

I never thought I would let her into the house; it was sacred. But when she showed up at our door when Erin was away, it was as if her energy were tumbling over the threshold, and if I didn't step aside, I'd be crushed in its path. She was coming in, and that was that.

She tried not to be obvious about it, but Irene's eyes were scanning the house like she'd just stepped inside Kirribilli House, a mansion. Everyone tried to act like it wasn't a big deal, coming here, but it was. Even to us, it still was; didn't make tragedy any easier to take. In a way, it made it worse. You were meant to be on top of the world if you had the luck to be in a place like this because it came with your big-time job—not just in some dickhead finance company, but in something that mattered. You'd taken the high road, and you still made it. Everyone knew the chances. And yet.

Well, I let her have her look, made like I didn't notice, but she stopped short four steps in, lifted her foot, and began unbuckling her sandal. She bounced a little on the other foot, and then looked at me, sheepish, and smiled. There she was. She put the naked foot down, and I could see her body melt. Whatever it was that had sent her reeling had gone warm and dripped out in a puddle. Her shoulders went limp. She stared at her foot for a minute, seemed to remember what she'd been doing, looked up, out the window, as if at a bird, and then very slowly, very thoughtfully, removed the other shoe.

"Right," she said, straightening up and shaking out her lovely (pastel!) hair.

She picked up her shoes and started to bolt for the door.

13

IRENE

I didn't belong there. The house itself was screaming that out to me. Butt out. This is not your place. You are just visiting. And aren't fancy enough for that, even in normal circumstances. Which this is not. Be polite and shut up. In fact, I felt the urge to bolt. No matter how attracted I was to Gavan, was it worth this upset?

"Wait!" Gavan pulled my arm. It was the most intimate moment we shared; it said, I know you well enough to pull your arm a little bit rough, and you know me well enough to see that I don't intend harm, only that you mean something to me and I don't want you to feel uncomfortable.

It was decided. I kept my mouth shut. We did understand each other, and I was meant to trust the part of me that said he didn't want to know. Whatever burden that created for me to carry, well, that would be my gift to him.

He was so gentle then, carried me to a bed, which I suspected was not the one he slept in. A strange thing, but respectful, exactly what I would have expected of him. I respected his wife, too. I wouldn't have been able to do the things that we did in her bed. Everything was deeper, intensified; something solidified between us there, and I knew I would never tell. Like it or not, I had too much to lose now.

"You can stay the night, if you like."

I looked at him, unsure.

"I would like you to."

How could I pass up the opportunity to stay here? "I would like to, too."

He kissed me on the nose. I laughed so hard I snorted. He seemed to enjoy that.

When the sun dropped, he left me to pick up some fresh fish for dinner. Of course he couldn't be seen leaving with me, and I was thrilled at the opportunity to be alone in the house for a few moments. I told myself I wouldn't snoop, but as I sat on the verandah, at the table with the Middle Eastern style tablecloth, I could feel my neck craning away from the beautiful, calm ocean, and back toward the house. Wouldn't there be clues in there? Maybe this was the answer: find out the truth of who knew what and ease my mind, and who knows? Maybe the whole problem goes away. Irene gets everything she deserves.

Erin Andrews's office was like a treasure chest: international coins in a ceramic dish with Italian writing on the side, framed bits of frayed fabric that looked ancient, books in every shape and size, arranged artfully with figurines and vases and intricate boxes poked in here and there. Even the lamp looked like it should be in a museum: Chinese and chipped, but with a pristine white shade. And then there were bits from Gavan's career: plaques and certificates framed on the walls. Emus and kangaroos and the rising sun. There was only one photo. The girl wasn't in it. Just Gavan and the wife, each with an arm alongside, but not quite touching, John Howard. Gavan's eyes were the same there as that day at BWS. What was this man thinking? Except for John Howard's face, I wouldn't have been able to guess if it was before or after what happened to the girl.

I ran my fingers over the loose pages on her desk. Without thinking, I removed the brass beetle paperweight and handled the top page. *You want to hear what happened to the girl. I understand. It's impossible to believe a thing like that could happen, so you want to hear about it over and over and over, but the truth is that no matter how many times you focus on the minute details, put it all together in a big picture, step back, and then sharpen your take, you're never going to know anything that makes sense of the thing . . .*

I heard a creak and panicked, slamming the beetle back over the stack with a thump. Standing stock still, I heard nothing else for a couple of minutes and poked my head back down toward the staircase. Gavan was nowhere in sight. Outside, the space for his car was still empty. I returned to the bedroom where the blankets were still unmade. One of my pink hairs was twirled on the pillow. The first time I saw that pale blonde-pink hair color, I knew I had to have it. It reminded me exactly of this long-petalled flower that grew each year along our front path. None of the other flowers Mum planted ever grew, but that one was lovely. My sister and I would lie with our chins in our palms and stare at it. We'd done it the first time to get a whiff, but it had no scent. The most beautiful flowers often have no scent, which seems like the devil's work. I did not feel like I was looking at that flower, nor that I was with my long-lost sister when I saw myself in the salon mirror and then paid $150, but a lovely serenity settled over me, and I liked it.

When I saw my hair on that expensive pillowcase, I pinched it and twirled it around my finger before putting it in my pocket. Even so, I got the sense that all of this—him, the house, whatever thing of his wife's I was about to read—was a dream. What was I *doing* here? There was Gavan's phone and his money clip and a few coins piled largest to smallest. Was I falling in love with him? It was doomed to go nowhere, and then where would I be? I couldn't help but picture a life with him: public appearances, rubbing shoulders with the governor general, wearing evening gowns and chignons with pearl earrings. No. I was a Band-Aid. I knew that. My fingers dipped in my pocket to feel for the hair. Held aloft, I let it slip to its full length, watched it spin in the light. No. I was not the kind of person who would steal someone else's life. Just in case, I twirled it up again and swallowed it, happy with the gesture, though I'd fight back gags for half an hour.

I tiptoed back to the notebook and read the whole thing.

14

MICK

Erin was meant to arrive in ten minutes. There was rosemary lamb sizzling out on the grill. A Sav Blanc was chilling. Whatever this game was, he was getting good at it.

Watching her produced surprising results: it addicted him to her. This was a woman who spent 99 percent of her time alone. And that 1 percent she spent with her husband, if her writing was accurate, was lonelier than the other 99. And yet, she hatched this plan, on her own, and though it clearly did not come naturally to her, she was going to follow through. Sure, he would be collateral if all went to plan, but he knew she wouldn't go through with it. Kiss, kill? Come on. He knew about that. Why was he alone in the first place? Krissy; she'd gotten the best of him. Knew how to push his buttons. It was their thing, initially. She'd tell him they were going to play out some scenario, like she didn't want him anymore, but then tell him to meet her at the bar, wink wink. They'd giggle. She was hot. Always up for it. Rubbing him under the table, forgetting to wear underwear. Probably she was always imagining he was someone else, doing something else to her, but this was part of it, the challenge, trying to get her to want *him*. He couldn't help himself.

And yet, there was always this anger sizzling just beneath the surface. Why *didn't* she love him for him? If she didn't, why didn't she just fuck off? The two sides of the argument were like heart and soul; they were inseparable. He told himself he could not have one without the other, and he would just have to deal or let her go, which he could not. He was sick with love for her. The moment he saw her, he wanted to peel off every item of her clothing and take her against a wall. He'd done it plenty, too. Restaurant loos, parking lots, even once right on a street, which in the moment he deemed desolate enough to go for it—not that he'd been thinking straight. The second it was over, he'd have to kiss her, suck on her ear, anything to hold onto that feeling for a bit longer. And she knew it, but she'd shimmy her skirt down, pull away, and often, ignore him the whole night afterward—even talk to other men, touching her hair, leaning in, flirting, while she made him sit at a nearby table and watch. It was part of the act, to keep this black magic, or whatever it was, going.

He'd show up, where she'd told him to meet her. Always he'd show up. Beforehand, she'd make him watch while she dressed—in some kind of lingerie that didn't have any structure, like a candy coating, or a bra with the crucial material cut out, tiny panties with a zipper he could undo to get what he wanted. Shit. Even now it killed him to think about it. He took a breath. That was in the past. He had something new that wasn't merely a house to work on. Erin/Erika was astounding in her own way, and he was going to take it where it led him. He owed her that much; he was a changed man with her. Never once angry in all the weeks he'd known her. Considered himself cured. He wasn't going to let that go.

Was he merely dazzled and not exactly in love? Probably. But he didn't mind. He hadn't planned to get this far again. And look what Erin/Erika was planning to do, and he didn't even have one angry bone in his body! It was more than a nice break; it was a precipice he was reaching the end of. Pretty soon he'd have to decide whether to jump or back down.

She wouldn't be able to kill him, obviously. Not if he was on guard, anyway. The problem was, what would he do when she tried? Would he wind up hurting her? Would this be a chance to tell her how he felt? How *did* he feel? This was the first time things had been so good, and he was bound to fuck it up. He'd told himself he hadn't been lonely, but that was horse shit, he knew. This woman *needed* him. And he would come through for her. That was the real test, of this he was sure.

15

AGGIE

Aggie treasured her hours behind the bar, even if she still got the worst shifts. There was an authority to it that seduced people into trusting her, believing she had intelligence. Much better than sitting in a uni tutorial, having some middle-aged woman with expensive shoes lord it over her for not giving feedback on some short stories. As if that was going to be the end of the world!

There were terrorists out there, and this woman wouldn't let her slide for allowing Kelly's not very subtly veiled stream of consciousness with conventionally unconventional punctuation about a girl she may or may not have had a crush on to go without someone telling Kelly, via some useless feedback form, that it could use more "original imagery" or some such "constructive feedback" that they were meant to use.

She took the class for an easy A, but you weren't allowed to say that when the tutor asked, were you? So she dropped it, and then the next one, until she was only registered in Urban Women's Issues, which, she'd fancied while she'd been browsing the catalog, sounded independent and irreverent, but had really been beyond her comprehension and interests. You all have vaginas, and men have dicks. There you go, folks! Must we endlessly discuss this? Shit. No wonder the world was in the state it was.

She'd been wearing that formless black shirt that slid off her shoulders by design when she'd seen that fancy woman's date— Mick!—come into the bar the first time, in his construction company T-shirt. She recognized the word *ProBuild* from trucks she'd seen around, and a billboard by the tracks. It was a couple years ago. She could tell there was something strange between him and the woman he was making eye contact with the whole night. For one thing, the woman wasn't wearing any underwear and wasn't all that discreet about it. Fucking gross. They'd have to burn that stool she was sitting on. And then there was the black eye she was trying to cover with her glasses and makeup. If you knew what to look for, there it was. They didn't sit together, and they didn't seem to like each other very much, but you could tell they were there for each other's benefit. She chatted to other blokes; he pretended not to watch, got more pissed off, drank more beers. A few times, he got up to go to the toilet, and Aggie thought he'd take out the guy she was talking to, let out a deep breath each time the toilet door swung behind him. It wasn't until later that there was trouble. The skank left with one of these guys, and Aggie didn't see exactly what happened out there by the parking spaces in front, but Ms. No Underwear had to take an ambulance from here, and the construction guy left in handcuffs. Fucking Mick.

Aggie couldn't believe it when he started coming back, like they were all family and would have to forgive him. How did he know they would? Why not go somewhere else where people didn't think you were an abusive son of a bitch?

Well, she wasn't going to tell that know-it-all woman about

that, was she? Reminded Aggie of that uni tutor. Better idea of what the world needs than everyone else, huh? Well, we'll see about that. Irene asked what Aggie knew about him—Mick—and she lied. Said she didn't know a thing about him. Irene was always messing up her life doing the right thing. Stay home with Mum so you can give her your salary to keep up with the expenses while Dad does fuck all. If she were Irene, she'd say to that fancy woman: Oh, grand idea! Why don't you go and fall in love with someone who everyone but you knows will beat the crap out of you, stuck-up bitch? Someone who thinks the world's there for his taking?

Yeah, Mick did have a secret, but it wasn't a wife, and that rich woman was the stupid one who'd next fall into his trap. Aggie had washed her hands of the whole thing. Don't need no Urban Women's Issues bitch to teach her that, now, did she?

16

ERIKA

She'd have to kill herself. Yes, obviously, there was no other way.

She'd been repeating the word *bludgeon* until it evoked a fat pigeon, but she knew she still couldn't do it. Weak, she'd thought. Weak, weak, weak. She was a pathetic person. Not an adult, actually, but the kind of person whom someone like her husband would have to save, someone who couldn't save themselves. Surely, she could set aside pedestrian worries like guilt and fear and physical disgust if she truly thought this would connect her to Olena.

Then it hit her: what if she *didn't* need to kill him at all? End of life, complete the cycle, yes, obviously. But why had she ever thought that ending this particular life was crucial? Yes, someone needed to die. It was clear—symmetrical, beautiful even. But why would it have to be him? It should be her. If he was reading these pages when she walked out after her coffee in a little while, he would have mercy on her, help her along even. Wouldn't he?

Yes. Without her realizing, the grotesque forensic vocabulary —putrefaction, incision, lesion; even a benign word like *body* in the wrong context—transformed from a stomach acher into something eloquent, a missing piece helping her to complete the circle.

Erika slid into the seat of her car. She'd watched Mick go around the side and fiddle with the patio slider with the dodgy lock until it pushed aside. They'd never enabled the security system. What the hell for? Who was going to get behind that iron gate? Who was going to get past the park's security guy sitting at the hill's precipice, drinking tea from a flask and listening to the rugby? Someone she'd left the gate open for— that was who.

The leather was hot on her exposed thighs. She knew he was aware of her watching, and that seemed like enough, so she drove away. She spent the day at the beach with the dog, and three hours later, she'd come back to get ready for her final evening with Mick. She hadn't expected the calm.

17

IRENE

What was I meant to do with the information? At first I was riveted. This was a compelling story. I couldn't put it down. My heart raced. With Gavan due to return at any moment, I read as much as I could. My fingers shook the pages; they swayed with my breath. My fingers smudged the ink, came away with words pressed into their grooves. I thought of Mother the whole time. How could I not? At its heart, this was a story about a mother's love. Even more so did I treasure those idiosyncrasies I knew of my own mother—me and no one else. Mother. Lovely, silly, arrogant Mother.

But I only reached the bit where Erika is speaking with Mick, and Gavan (*Gav*, as she calls him, like a different person altogether) pulls up to the traffic light, when Gavan pulled up right outside the window where I sat, turning into the carport. It gave me chills to see him on the page, through her eyes, and then simultaneously, here, the iron gate rolling shut slowly behind him.

Trembling, I scraped the pages into order and bounced the

edges on the desktop to straighten them. Carefully, I returned them to where they'd been found and ran back to the bedroom to splay myself on the bed. But as I posed, I wondered, had he seen these words? Why had she left them so openly?

"He*llo*," he sang up, nearly giddy. "I have croissants. I have black coffee."

My heart jumped. Our connection had thickened.

"Up here," I said, the opposite of giddy. Serious, probably as serious as I'd ever been. As I heard his footfalls, I changed my position, pulled my legs together, turned on my side, and propped my head up on one elbow. My hair slipped down my shoulders. The natural light in this room was dense, palpable. Probably it was something to do with the ocean's reflection. I watched the surface of it as I heard him approach.

I turned to him as he entered the room.

"Oh," he said. In his hands were a bag and a cardboard tray with two takeout coffee cups. He let the bag fall to his side, and his mouth twitched, as if a weaker man would have let it go slack.

He put everything on the side table, knocking over his coins, removed his shirt, sat to remove his boots. His strength was visible, as if he wasn't just muscular, but charged up, ready to power the world if it needed him to do so. By the time he stood, I could see his erection. My breath caught. He saw me look and respond, and clearly this turned him on. God, being a woman could be a mighty thing. He reached for my hand, pulled me to my knees at the edge of the bed. Our lips hovered, nearly touching. I was breathless. *You are a straight line.* Yes, and this was precisely what enticed me. A straight line in the middle of all this. A straight line with a rigid perpendicular line shooting out your underwear. Hee hee. *Show, don't tell.* I had no idea what it meant, though he'd explained it to me twice, but I did my best to interpret. I wanted him to overtake me, and so I tried not to move even a centimeter. I was before the pink flower, and I would not harm it. Geraldine, wherever you are, sister, you would be proud.

It worked. He pressed his lips, his chest, his hardness to me. A moan escaped me. Something clenched inside, and I felt everything drop, go liquid. Just like that, he unbuckled his belt, his jeans fly, and revealed himself. The shaft pressed against me. I quivered. He repositioned, and there was the tip of him. No, no. This is not a good idea. And yet ideas had nothing to do with it. He was pushing. And then he was in. On my back, I slid my legs as wide open as they would go. I wanted him all the way. And then release circuited somewhere key inside me. I pulsed around him, taking him in tighter. "Fuck," he said, and then there was wet on my stomach.

He collapsed onto his back and pulled me onto his chest, kissed my forehead. Safe. It was the safest I'd ever felt. If he couldn't give this to Erin any longer, then they were broken. Very broken. When was the last time they'd fucked like that? If she was moving on to a new world, then perhaps he was too, here with me. Or maybe I was nothing to him, a push-button release. Still, he didn't seem the type.

He reached to the side table, grabbed the drinks, passed one to me.

"Thanks."

"You're most welcome."

"Hey, Gav?"

He started at the nickname. Sat up. Shit.

"I think I need to get back to work after we eat," he said.

18

AGGIE

That little minx! Aggie couldn't believe her friend had it in her. Good on her for sleeping with that bitch's husband. Watching them had turned her on. The window facing the parking lot was small, so she saw only a rectangle of their skin touching, but in a way this was more personal, focusing from this angle on one small spot, a view which even they never got to see. She had to drag her eyes away and force herself to reverse out of the museum parking space. She wasn't a peeping Tom, after all.

The following week, she decided what to do. She wouldn't ruin Irene's good time by involving her. Instead, she'd get the wife in trouble by telling her husband about the affair. She knew about men's double standards. But how would she approach him? Who would she say she was? Why would she say she was telling him? Because . . . because she was probably in danger, his wife, and Aggie had to let him know before it was too late.

But why not just keep it to herself and let Micko hurt the

wife? Surely, at some point he would. But this way, the woman would suffer for sure. She'd lose everything, and maybe Irene would get everything instead. Yes, that appealed to her sense of justice. Irene was a lovely girl. She deserved everything, and Aggie would give it to her. Micko and the whore be fucked.

19

ERIKA

In the shower, she takes extra time. Shaves what little hair she has, then decides that maybe she will shave off everything. There is a sense of crescendo. After, she looks in the mirror at her bare self. The frankness feels right. Almost beautiful. She is art. Perfect.

She pulls on the slip and the dress, white, white. Pins up her hair. Pearl earrings, lipstick. But beyond the dressing table, out the window, is a girl parked in a car in front of the museum who captures her attention. It is the bartender. She feels rattled. The girl is watching her. She knows this because as soon as she catches her eye, the girl looks away, starts the engine, and drives off.

Erika is rattled as she drives to Micko's. If this girl has been watching Erika, then what else does she know? And who else knows? No, no. She cannot know about the murder plot. How would she? But wait. It wouldn't matter if she knows because Erika will be dead in a few hours if all goes to plan. But what if it doesn't? She is going to have to depend on Micko more than ever to have mercy on her and let her go and die if that's what she wants. They will make it look like suicide so he will not be blamed. She should write a note. Why hadn't she thought of this before? A note to absolve him. She pulls over and starts writing.

Dear

And already she is stumped. Is she writing this to Gavan? And if so, then should she explain what she is doing here? Self-ish. She knows he hasn't read the pages, doesn't set foot in her office. She cannot do this to Gavan. Pantsing. It is wonderful, but it is also reckless because you can't predict what will happen until you are in situ.

It must be written to Gavan.

Dear Gavan,

Here I am, trying to say the unsayable. Show, don't tell. Surely you have heard me say this, back when we had things to say. A straight line cannot tell you what I have done here. You are a straight-line man, and so I know this is difficult to understand. But you do have imagination. You are inspired by strength and have shown incredible sympathy even if you aren't always able to put yourself in others' shoes, because you have seen too much to be compassionate about those who fall outside your code. Which I am afraid I do. I do not say that to gain your compassion. In fact, I believe you are as compassionate with me as you are able—have pushed yourself in this direction beyond the limits of most humans. Know I appreciate it. Know I blame you for nothing; in fact, it is the opposite: I blame me. I do not say this lightly. I will not use worn-out euphemisms to diminish what happened to our daughter and our reactions to it. Let the art speak for me. Let the art become me. I have already become the art. And this is the best outcome. Go. Start again. It is what I am doing, in my way. The pages are on my desk. Read them. Read me. I will not use the L-word. What we have is more and less and different and ours always.

Forever, Erika

He will understand the name when he reads the story. She tucks the page and the pen beneath her handbag on the leather passenger seat and continues to her destination. She no longer feels selfish. She feels like destiny fulfilling itself. Everything lined up perfectly.

20

AGGIE

She'd done it. A weight felt lifted. Her next stop was Micko's house. Yes, she knew where it was. She'd been there. He was a slightly rough fuck. But she'd liked it. She wanted more, but he pretended not to know her the next time he'd shown up at the bar. Dick. She'd always suspected he was bad news, but that confirmed it. Unfortunately, seeing his wife with the black eye had only challenged her. She could take him, even if that woman couldn't. She was strong. Yeah, right.

So. She didn't know exactly why she was at Micko's except for vague feelings of doom and duty. As a citizen, she probably should have told Irene about the woman with the black eye. She probably should have just told that woman the day she'd asked, that Micko was a good lay, but dangerous. If nothing else, her expression would have been priceless. But there was such a thing as justice, and this time, it was in her hands. She could decide who knew what, and she liked that. Especially if it meant that Micko might be fucked over as a result.

She slid into a spot where Micko's street curved, so that from the house itself, she couldn't be seen. It was as if the spot were put there for exactly this purpose. For a long time, nothing happened. She was getting bored and had eaten too many cheese Twisties. They were beginning to repeat on her.

Finally, the woman, who she'd been pretty sure had recognized her parked out front of the museum earlier, emerged now from around the corner. She walked in Aggie's direction, until she turned up Micko's walk, which was sandwiched between swaths of fresh dirt, from which small shrubs were putting down roots. The woman didn't seem to see Aggie, who watched as she made her way up the three steps to the porch familiarly. Aggie had been so drunk when she'd been here that she'd tripped over the bottom one and scratched her knee. There was still a jagged, shiny scar.

He made her wait a moment after she pressed the bell. Aggie could see him watching the woman from the staircase landing above, which had a large window overlooking the walkway and front steps. Dick. Then he hurried down the stairs and opened the door. In the light of the entry, the woman looked glamorous, in pristine white. Mick looked her up and down, as if she were for sale, and even from this distance, she could tell he liked what he saw. Was she jealous?

He led her inside and closed the door. Now Aggie couldn't see anything. She sat like that for another ten minutes. *Closer.* She had to get out of the car and get closer. Maybe she *was* a peeping Tom. Swiftly, she closed the door, walked the block as if she belonged there, in case anyone was watching, and then turned into the driveway and took a seat at the bench that gave her a view through the kitchen and dining room windows. The branches on the tree overhead were low enough that she felt concealed.

21

GAVAN

He hated that woman with the short haircut right from the start. Why was she meddling? What did she have to gain from telling him that his wife was having an affair? It should have surprised him more. But he was a pragmatic man. They'd had sex exactly three times since Olivia died. All three were desperate, clutching affairs, grunts and thrusts designed to fuck through everything. For a second, each of them worked. After one particular time, they'd gotten drunk on dark rum and lay in bed until noon the following day, which was the one time he'd ever called in sick. But the next day was back to reality. Their family had been smashed. If God had any sympathy, he would have taken them all out in one go. But if God was anything, he was a motherfucker.

No, Gavan wasn't angry about the affair. But he was incredibly jealous. If he couldn't have his wife, why should some other fucker have her? Okay, so he *was* also angry. And getting angrier the more he thought about it. Yes, one could obviously make the point that he had Irene. But he didn't know what to make of her. Sometimes it made him sick to think of how young she was and whether he was having some kind of Freudian crisis here. All he knew was that there was something uncomplicated and purely pleasurable about his time with her. And afterward, he felt like a disgusting, selfish prick for about ten minutes, until he told himself to harden the fuck up and just think of it as a means of survival, a way to get by. Feelings aside. It worked. When he wasn't with Irene, he locked her up in a corner of his mind and didn't go anywhere near her.

But now his wife was doing it too. And he wouldn't have it. Disgraceful. What if other people had seen her? This was Australia, not America, and no one would bring it up, obviously. No one would ask him to talk about how it made him feel. But they'd know. And he'd know they knew. A man whose wife fucked other men. What would that make him? Weak. There was no way around it. Who was going to respect him if his own wife didn't? Nah.

Dignity. That was what he needed to use to attack this situation. He would confront her and tell her to stop it immediately. If she had respect for him, she would. But what if she didn't have respect for him? What if she thought the way he'd continued on through life, as if there hadn't been any other choice, had been the action of a weak man, and she'd lost all respect for him, the way he had of himself? Soldier on. The words sounded embarrassing to him now. He'd used them as a way to escape what he hadn't been able to deal with. And now he was fucking a girl who wasn't much more than a teenager. His wife might even know. And now she was going to leave him for another man.

He went in her office and ransacked it. But what he'd been looking for was right on her desk. He recognized the pile of papers. She'd left them there in the open this whole time. Had she wanted him to read them? Had she wanted him to save her from this? Had he again failed miserably?

He sat at her desk, fingers gripping the lovely, thick paper, with its expensive weave. She was so elegant, Erin (Erika, as she thinly veiled herself in the story). The first story of hers that she'd let him read was about a girl who kisses a man for two hours without letting him put his hands on her body. In the end, the girl walks away and giggles with her friends, pointing at the man when they next see him walking in front of the shop where the girls hang out. He said it was cruel. Erin said it was true. And that it was about the difference between girls, who think they have power over men, and women, who realize it is men who have the power, and that girls put themselves in danger by ever believing differently. In the end, the woman is much older, letting her husband have sex with her though he repulses her. After, she makes him tea. Gav had argued this was a negative view of the world, but he knew she was right. Mostly, she was right.

This, from a woman who had always had power over him. He'd done his best to convince her of the opposite throughout their marriage, but it was true to this day, obviously.

But what to make of the supernatural bits of the story? Memento mori. Connecting with their daughter? Even as he grunted, he felt himself wanting to believe. You never stopped irrationally believing you'd see those olive eyes again. The mismatched socks and backward, misbuttoned shirts that he'd never had the heart to correct. Erin's deeper insight had always been a force of his attraction. Despite himself, he wanted to believe. Of course he did. He obviously wasn't the only pathetic hopeful. Wasn't this the kind of outlandish miracle that religion and art based themselves on? In the end, there may be something more. Right-o.

So what? Let his wife kill herself? Or force her to live miserably for his benefit, which, let's face it, was no longer very beneficial? Soldier on? If it had been a military exercise, there'd be rules, and therefore no question. But it wasn't.

22

ERIKA

Micko's place smelled like Christmas. That was what Gav would have said. He'd been using that phrase so much in their brief exchanges, it was driving her mad. If their words were so limited, why use clichés? But the saying was growing on her all the same. Lamb was sizzling, confirming he'd read the pages (or that he liked to cook lamb). So, their first look said, we both know what we know. But she was nearly bluffing because she didn't have a plan to get him to kill her. She was pantsing this bit, but could pantsing be considered a plan? It had gotten her this far, and she was pretty sure she couldn't have worked this out beforehand.

He took in her dress, top to toe, removed her white jacket at the front door, began sliding the hem of her skirt up with his splayed fingers. So, it was going to be like this? Shockingly, she found herself incredibly turned on. At the precipice of what would come next, it was as if the old had been erased and there was only this moment. Which was precisely what she had been wanting all this time. She gave herself over to it.

Micko slammed the door shut and pushed her up against it. His eyes were closed tightly as he entered her, and they both came quickly. No one bothered about protection. What would be the point? She felt him come inside her and took that, too, as a sign of their understanding. A dead woman cannot have a baby. When their breathing relaxed, his eyes opened, and he kissed around the back of her neck, where his head had been resting. He clutched her tightly before loosening his grip and helping her to straighten up.

She took a seat on the couch, next to the lamp, and asked him for a glass of wine. While his back was turned, she sized up the diameter of the lamp to see if her memory of it had been accurate.

When he returned, Micko sat next to her, staring at the lamp. She stared at him, waiting for him to call it off. Now would be the moment, wouldn't it? But he said nothing. Moved closer to her, starting kissing her ear. She responded, this time taking the lead, pulling down her panties and straddling him.

As she took him in, he groaned and whispered something that sounded like, "I love you."

She stopped.

"What did you say?"

"I said I love you."

Their noses were nearly touching. He braced her hips and pushed himself deeper.

She tried to pull back, but he wouldn't let her. "Why would you go and do something like that?"

He shrugged. "Didn't plan for it."

Her shoulders slumped. She gazed at the ceiling, then jerked her face back his way. "Then you'll do it."

"I can't."

"Please."

"It's crazy."

"Crazy? What do you know about art? You're a builder."

"Don't do that."

"What?"

"Try to anger me so that I do it."

"At what point did you get to know me so well?"

"You're a wonderful writer. I have never known anyone better."

"Then do it."

"Dying is not going to take you to your daughter."

"How do you know?"

"Because it's rubbish."

"Even if it is rubbish, the art will stand and make people think about the kind of world we created that let something like that happen to Olena."

"Will it? People don't even read anymore."

"Don't say that."

"It's the truth. Don't you want the truth? For Olivia?"

She shuddered. For him to use the name. It was a red line. She knew what she had to do. "What good is that? We each live our own truth."

"You can run away from everything and make our life together your truth."

"It doesn't work that way."

"Well, it doesn't work the way you think it does, either."

He was still inside her, and he thrusted. She closed her eyes, again, the moment taking precedence. She was so close to whatever was next, she could taste it. If it took words to get Micko to do what she wanted, she could get there. She was excellent with words.

He thrust again.

Now she felt herself waiting for more. She pushed against him, but he wouldn't move. It was a game. She pushed and pushed, and he began to moan, and again he came inside her.

Life inside her. But she didn't finish, and so she pushed more. She was close now. Then there. She heard herself moaning. And then footsteps. Closer up the walk. She didn't pay it much mind because she hadn't written anyone else in. Though Micko's use of her name had sent her worlds colliding.

The door flew open.

"Gav!" She jumped up, straightening her skirt.

She felt as if she were seeing her husband in combat. She'd heard a few stories from his friends, when they'd been drinking, but she hadn't been able to picture it. Especially when she knew how much they all embellished. But this was the image that had eluded her: he was all business. She almost couldn't recognize him. They were his features, but with no give. More like a welder's mask made to resemble him. Micko was strong, but he either wasn't trying or didn't have a chance. His arms barely flapped. He still had an erection.

She heard herself yell, "No! No!"

Gav's hands were around Micko's neck, squeezing. This would be the worst possible outcome: if she hurt everyone around her. "No! Don't kill him."

She did all she could think to do: she picked up the lamp, which was heavier than she'd suspected, and used the wide top, rather than the narrow bottom, to hurt, but not kill, Gav, so that he'd let Mick go. She was disgusted at the feeling of satisfaction that striking the blow instilled: had she blamed him somehow for what had happened to Olena? It was illogical. The fault was not his, but still, here she was. She could not deny the feeling, blooming there amid the panic and care for him.

The force of the blow was enough for Gav to drop his hands and stumble back onto the coffee table. Mick's hands went right to his throat. He gasped and then coughed and eventually sighed as great breaths tumbled through his passageway.

They were in a sort of circle, chests heaving, taking in the scene, what had happened. Footsteps again, the door crashing against the wall. The bartender.

It was clear from Micko's response that he knew her.

23

AGGIE

She could never get enough of the story. In it, she came off like an angel, a savior. And in the end, that was how it had turned out. But it wasn't what she intended when she burst through the door. She didn't know *what* she had in mind.

She was outside looking in, and then all of a sudden, she was part of the action. Immediately, she sensed she'd made a mistake. This wasn't her story. She'd crossed some sort of line. She was worse than a peeping Tom. At least those guys stuck to the rules.

Micko's look said it all. *What the fuck are you doing here?*

She'd been binge-watching this unfold, and she had to know the ending. Now all she wanted was to run back to her spot under the tree, but it was clearly too late for that now.

"Please don't call the police," the woman said to her.

She hadn't even considered it. But now she saw she held the power. It changed things. She took them all in: Micko, who'd fucked her over, the bitch who had it coming, the bigwig who everyone knew, who'd looked at her like a maggot when she'd dobbed in his wife. And yet, she had it over all of them. So, what would she do now?

She waited too long. Gavan was up again, this time with the pointy end of the lamp, and he yielded it like a weapon and smashed Micko in the skull once, twice, three times.

Micko put his hands to his head. His fingers came away covered in inky dark blood. He had to pull his fingers away because Gavan kept smashing, as if he were possessed and couldn't stop even if he wanted to.

Micko was probably dead after the fifth time, but Gavan kept hefting the lamp and making contact with Micko's skull, which made the most disgusting wet sound, as if it had gone liquid.

She nodded once so they'd both see, and then she turned around and left. She would never tell. It was the only thing to do, and it had been clear to all of them. She didn't know how it was all handled, but Micko's death was never linked to Gavan. It was a small town, and he was considered a good person and Micko was not. And the only people who knew they bore any connection were Aggie and Irene.

Looking back, she'd done the right thing, telling Gavan, then keeping everything to herself. She even grew to admire the woman. She was strong, did what she had to do. Aggie could respect that.

Irene moved away. She suspected her friend had been in love with Gavan. But in the end, Aggie had probably helped her, too. Because he was never going to be with Irene in any real way, and she would have wasted who knows how long in pursuit. Last Aggie heard, she was in Brussels. There'd been a bomb blast. A real one. She didn't know whether Irene had been there, but she'd never heard from her again.

Gavan and his wife moved on to a new posting. The house was painted yellow. Everything looked different now. Still, whenever Erin put out a new book, she read it. It was easy to find out, even though she put them out anonymously, because the media made a huge deal, trying to guess her identity. Always the plot revolved around a senseless death. Like a literary serial killer. They were not bestsellers, but they made waves, made people think, and for a few weeks after, she thought people were kinder, more careful, giving. But maybe that was just her imagination.

The first one came out a year after the murder. It gave her chills to hear the story as fiction, to hear herself named Katarina, to hear how respected her discretion had been. Noble, was how she saw herself after that reading.

She'd gone to the bookshop in a disguise. Her hair was that pinky-blonde Irene's had been at the time this had all gone down, cut to shoulder length, with an edgy, razored finish. She wore a white dress and a white coat and told herself Erin's words, which she'd inscribed over the book-signing table, with only the most cursory of glances at Aggie, but a glittering smile, were a thank-you: *Memento mori*, she'd written.

She'd walked out of that bookshop and drove right to the bar to tell her boss where to shove her job. She was going to do something that would help people. Clearly, this was her calling. How was she to know the next book would be about her? The bare wires. Why would she touch them? Because Erin's words, when she finally answered Aggie's letter, were that powerful. Now that she'd been invited back, she couldn't have kept away from the scene of the crime if she'd tried.

COMING SOON...

AN EXCERPT FROM THE NEXT INSTALLMENT OF THE GIRL IN THE
BOOK SERIES:

PROLOGUE

You want to know what this book's about, don't you? You've read
the blurb, deciphered the cover, seen a few newspaper write ups.
You're intrigued, and even feeling clever about the way you
understand instinctively how to balance the reader reviews to

account for trolls, friends, and bonafide readers. Yes, yes, it's a psychological thriller, but it's also about books and reading. There's a disappearance that can't be easily explained. A family at risk. Well, that's all well and good. But can't you just say exactly what it's *about*? Sorry, no. To paraphrase Flannery O'Connor, the meaning of a story does not rise to the top of a book like schmaltz in a soup pot. A story is not a textbook. As she so eloquently put it, "the whole story is the meaning." Try putting that in a blurb.

It is better to think of a book like a wonderfully engineered car driving through a new land with no itinerary. And no roads. The good news is Reader can wind up with an excellent guide. It is possible to recognize an excellent guide immediately. If this guide can show Reader a character who travels back in time along a telephone connection and Reader buys it, hook, line, and sinker, then he can be confident he has an excellent guide. He knows the rules, this guide, and he can choose which to follow and which to bend because he knows what's important about these rules and why. He knows he can make anything happen, because in the story, it is the experience that matters. But to Reader, everything is so dazzling, this is easy to forget. The journey is eye-opening. The brain is careening off in different directions. As Reader is propelled along these roads, he feels himself changing. Wanting to try that Indonesian dish mentioned in The Novel. Interested in taking a tour of Perugia, like the heroine has. Skinny-dipping in a neighbor's pool at midnight. There is something not-quite-right about the way Reader is glued to all he encounters in The Novel, and yet, at the same time, aches to race through the pages to see where it is he's going to. But Reader realizes, if he does that, gobbles it all up ravenously, it will be over too soon.

And suddenly it is. Abruptly, like a tumble with lots of bruis-ing. And that's when the question haunts most: which is the reality? The dazzling, eye-opening journey that sent Reader's heart racing, or this lonely bedroom, where Reader faces a pile of unwashed laundry and an alarm clock that will go off with such monotonous regularity in a few hours that Reader doesn't even need it anymore to signal the start of another soul-destroying day? Surely, there must be something more to it all than that. How to harness the magic of the story and keep it when the alarm bell rings? Well, I've got the answer, fuckers. No one would believe it if I told them. So I don't.

I

As a child, it all seemed innocuous enough. Mother drilled the same words into me as she buttoned me up at the front door: "Do you have your book? Always carry a book with you, so you can ground your reading experience in real life," she'd say. How cultured. How well-rounded.

"But why-*uh*?" I wanted to know. I'd stopped plugging my ears with my fingers long ago.

"Never mind why-uh. Like most things in this life, you have to work it out for yourself." I was six; I had my book, but often no snack or extra underwear. I assumed she thought I'd eventually find a way to read myself out of sopping pants. I never doubted she loved me, but she was specific about what was important (books), and was self-contained, as if she'd still be whole without me, and didn't that make me feel I needed her all the more?

"Mom! Mom!" I'd yell once she'd turn and head for the school gates.

"What is it?"

But it was never anything. I wanted everyone to see. This formidable woman was my mother.

My readiness would get tested, the way we did in school for atomic bomb explosions. On line at the echoey bank, below the gothic ceiling, I'd ask, "Can I have some goldfish?" She'd fish in her purse for a moment before saying, "Sorry darling. I forgot them. Do you have your book?"

"Do you have *your* book?" I'd ask when I felt stroppy. But she ignored such things. She knew I didn't mean them and I didn't need to apologize.

Between the queue's velvet ropes, my mind careening between the exact likeness of my hair—dark, thick, and ropy— to Mother's, though hers was braided and mine in two ponytails, and those square cushions of bubblegum in the machine at the door. I watched as another girl's mother pinched a penny out of her pocket and handed it to her hopping daughter, who carefully placed it in the slot and, practiced, cupped her hand beneath the chute as she turned the dial that set the gum cascading.

I pulled a face but Mother wouldn't look at me.

What could I do but start reading my book?

———

Beneath the gaze of those capacious eyes, her dark features at their most severe, my face tingled, my stomach lurched.

"I'm not messing around, Millie," was something she liked to say.

I distinctly remember suffering a minor bladder failure at such a moment at that bank, and tying the arms of my ski jacket around my waist to hide it. This wasn't a woman who needed to say, My way or the highway. She'd have to turn people away because of crowding at the Road Not Travelled, where I could have made a fortune selling Depends to bladder-challenged six year-olds, so they could all make a good, dry impression on her.

"Remove that ear from your mouth and speak up," was another thing she said, referring to what she liked to call 'your father's guilty-conscience plush beagle,' whose ear was always soggy between my front teeth that year. Mother's tone was plainly less Land of Make-Believe than do or die. As if to detract attention from my dripping pant leg, a croak escaped, vibrating the matted toy between my lips.

I mastered the art of carrying my book around, had one of her old satchels for the purpose. God, I loved the worn canvas of that thing, sucked its strap almost as much as the dog's ear. By the time I was in junior high school, I was wearing ribbed turtle-necks and vintage floral skirts, my nose in a book by my own accord. Emulating her containment, I amassed my own admir-ers, who didn't realize I was all show.

Even the show crumbled soon enough. When I pretended to master the magnificence of books (err, have one with you, act like you understand why), she started in on something else.

"How do you know what's real, Millie?"

I always offered the wrong answer. She wouldn't speak to me all afternoon so I could take time to work it out. Which I wouldn't. I often took my dinner alone. It would have been too juvenile, too much of a failure in her eyes for me to hate her.

And so it began.

It would be many years until I knew why, and exactly how much you must trust that eventually everything will come together to make sense, and perhaps most importantly, until I understood exactly why Mother was so focused on separating fact from fiction, but in the meanwhile, the learning curve made me into a clever party trick.

"Tell them," Mother would say.

At least I felt special then: no one else in that room knew Mother took this *where I read this book* show seriously, none of them suspected she was up to anything the way I already did—even if I didn't know exactly *what*. I would tell them all, in my frilly dress with its floral sash, that *Jane Eyre* is forever entangled with the rear-facing back of our Volvo station wagon, and *Robinson Crusoe* with the small electrics department of Bloomingdale's Lexington Avenue. I'd heard Mother recount my performances, and these were proud words she used. I didn't understand them all but I sounded lovely when she spoke of me that way.

This was all before the divorce, and of course I never noticed how this act drove my father out of the conversation. I just listed off these book/life associations and soaked up the attention: "*Are You There God? It's Me Margaret* and spaghetti carbonara," I would say, eventually, getting the dramatic pause right. "*Bedknobs and Broomsticks* and Intercourse, at the Pennsylvania Dutch Country."

Our flashy neighbors and the trio my father referred to as Mother's holdover hippie college friends laughed into a cloud of menthol cigarette smoke and started to sing out their own pairings. When the comments became more obviously inappropriate for a girl my age, Mother assumed I wouldn't understand, and chortled along with "Anais Nin and furry handcuffs," shooting me barely a glance over her gin and tonic. But even if the Intercourse double entendre was above my head, I sensed what this last comment meant. By ten, I'd read the slim volume with the bow-topped, mary-janed girl on the cover, and terrifyingly, felt my body respond. Books had taught me everything. Even—if I'd noticed, which was hard to do in the shadow of Mother—why someone like my father would be hunched awkwardly in the corner, fumbling with the pull-tab of his Budweiser. Alienation is a novelist's pet theme.

I didn't stop to think why any of it was important, but it certainly made Mother happy. And back then that made everyone happy. Even my alienated father—for a while anyway. This is where it starts to sound depressing. But, I never think of it that way. I don't give in to depression. I think of how my father used to say to me, "Some of us don't have the *luxury* of being depressed," though he'd never dare say that to Mother, and it made me hate him a little when he tried the phrase on my ears. Even still, we don't get to choose what affects us, do we?

Instead of giving in, I concentrated: these words of Mother's about reality and grounding books into the real world have come to mean a great deal to me, because they were among her last. After the second time she tried to kill herself, eighteen years ago, Mother stopped speaking. This followed the first suicide attempt, when Mother swallowed her Prozac supply and nodded off reading her favorite Lorrie Moore short fiction. I remember my fifteen-year-old self thinking bravo, how well you've grounded that book forever in our lives. How could I ever top that? Didn't I spend time trying to come up with an answer. Again, we can't help what really gets to us, though Lord knows I've tried.

Leading to that first time, she'd spent days of her life trying to work out how a writer could be so articulate, could get everything so beautifully, painfully, right. And then there she was, the print transferred onto her face where she'd let the book rest, her vomit adhering the words to her in a whole new way. If my marvelous friend Angie, who was always troublingly attached to Mother, and I had found her—our mouths agape, our constant attentions evidently failures—even seconds later, she'd have died then and there. As it stood, the vomit had blocked most of her airway.

"You saved her life, girls," the EMT with the immaculately groomed goatee had said to us as we rode along to the hospital; he called her puking *emesis* and patted our backs hard in a reassuring way I wasn't used to. Still, my best friend and I weren't convinced. We thought our schemes at enlivening post-divorce Mother had not only been a failure, but perhaps had landed her here. How many times had she asked, "Just leave me alone girls, please"?

After the divorce and before the first suicide, when I spent hours hovering over her, drinking ginger ale through bending straws and trying to beg her off the sofa, she'd say, "Millie, show, don't tell." I already knew the basics of fiction craft, though I probably couldn't name off the full fifty states. Mother had a book in her. I grew up knowledgeable of that fact. "If only we could medically remove it," my father would say to me in confidence sometimes, after he let me pull the ring on his Budweiser for that satisfying *carbon discharge.*

But in those days she spent lying in bed or watching reruns of *The Love Boat,* it was as if I couldn't hear Mother at all. I saw what I wanted her to be and I'd just rant, ticking off items on my own agenda, in order to get her there. "Why don't you just get up and *do* something?" I'd yell. "And how about drinking some *juice* instead of ginger ale for a change (what an example I was setting sliding my own Canada Dry can behind my back)? Remember fruit? You used to be *Mrs.* Fruit—"

"*Ms.*"

"Oranges and mangos, and people even juice strawberries now, I hear you can do bananas with the right attachment." We didn't have any of the attachments and we both knew it. We had a juicer, but it was buried in the basement with the other wedding gifts Mother had been granted in the divorce. I used to look at them so differently than I do now—as artifacts that could tell the story of what went wrong. I was a natural optimist, always looking to solve the problem. *If only we could medically remove it.*

"I'm just not that kinda girl anymore," Mother said without a shred of nostalgia.

But I was hungry for the old days, in awe of the way meaning changes over time; all those hopeful countertop appliances. We weren't those people now; I was starting to wonder if we ever were. I didn't think Mother *did* ever have a book in her. *Ms.* Fruit didn't have much to say at all.

But I didn't say that—it would've just been more telling, likely; instead, what I'd do to *show* Mother was get up and dance the tango while sipping cranberry juice out of one of the Star Wars glasses from Burger King—usually the Princess Lea—and Mother would actually laugh. More satisfying than the Budweiser carbon discharge. God, I loved to hear her shocking cackle.

"I'll say one thing for you, you've got a wonderful sense of humor," she said once, as if it were a magnificent gift. Sometimes she'd cry a little after and say, "Get your old mom a tissue, would you?" My shoulders would go rigid with her compliment, I'd carry the tissue like a knight's sword, but I'd wonder why my humor, if it was so wonderful, wasn't enough. Was there anything I could ever show that *would be* enough?

True to the EMT's words, Mother lived, but no longer was she the woman who'd fallen asleep reading of a faded starlet in a

Midwestern motel who somehow touched the tender spot of Mother's own troubles. This personality byte had gone the way of the juicer. Somewhere in the transaction—the reading, the pills, the vomit, the crossing over, the crossing back—Mother had abandoned her depression somewhere, like a left duffle bag on a train platform.

I should have been thrilled to leave all that behind. But without it, I had to get to know her all over again. And not in the way Angie and I had hoped during all those years plying her with outlandish proposals for physical activity.

It wasn't that she'd become happy, only flat. Perhaps the worst surprise of all though, was that she didn't seem to need me in the way she had. I could stay in my room all day, smoking cigarettes I pretended to want and like, and she wouldn't notice my absence—never mind the smoke; I think she ignored that on purpose—until she was off to bed herself.

Suddenly my father's catchphrase from my childhood took on a new sense: "Beware a well-read woman," he used to say whenever Mother said the thing about carrying a book. I'd never understood this comment—and to overcompensate, laughed each time I'd heard it; surely a woman and a book could be nothing but harmless; just look at all those men with their guns, Mother used to say. And that made sense to me. Now she was gone, the words rolled through my head like a ticker.

———

After the second botched suicide, she'd been transferred to New Jersey General Hospital's psychiatric wing, far from our Long Island home, but where she'd spent time twice before—after the divorce, and then after the first suicide. Thirty days later, stumped by her loss of speech, and threatened by me for the questionable ethics of their treatments, the doctors released to my custody a silent Mother. I'll never forget the way she looked sitting in my passenger seat, her hands folded on her lap, waiting for me to strap her in, as if this type of thing—an ordinary car ride—was no longer a part of her world. I couldn't help myself, and kissed her on the cheek after I'd leaned through the open door to click the belt. She looked at me and smiled. It was the last time she'd do so.

At first it was nerve-wracking, the silence. There were days so quiet I would forget I could speak myself. Every sound became a feature: the crunch of a chip, the tinkle of a fork. When I turned on the hi-fi, I had to dial the sound real low, volume had become unbearable. I wanted to hate her. What the fuck was she doing to our lives? But I'd catch a glimpse of her through her office door, after the second suicide, so studious with her blackboards and her books, and I felt overwhelmingly that she was being the only person she could be. I didn't hate her, despite Dr. Weiner my therapist advising me it was okay to do so. You don't know her, I'd say. But eventually, the ways in which I, as witness, might translate this experience engorged my senses. For the first time, I felt I wielded some power.

Unlike the inertia following the first suicide, she now had me drive her to rare bookshops, whose addresses she'd rip out of the Yellow Pages and circle in runny black pen. She'd schlep a tote bag to the library in some of her old Parisian getups—all this *action*, so different from her years on the sofa—but this time as I watched her purposefully scanning the card catalogs, I was thinking that surely her speech would return at any moment, this woman so fond of words. What book was she looking for? Whatever it was, she didn't seem to find it. Always, she'd come out deflated and empty-handed. After such a trip, I once drove to The Olde Ice Cream Parlor—the one with the old Singer sewing machine tables, where you could pump the iron foot pedal while you waited for your root beer float.

When I pulled the car to a stop in front, I thought I'd done something right. She smiled. But when I turned the car off, she wouldn't budge. *"Wuthering Heights,"* I said. In the gloaming, the outlines of the naked trees terrifying and beautiful in the foreground over the old town shop fronts, Mother spoke her single, last words. "Yes. You've got it. Finally."

"What? What did I get?"

Nothing.

"I read that here, yes. But so what? What could that possibly matter now?"

I couldn't decide if she was an asshole or the smartest woman in the world. It was a bold statement, her lack of statement, but she weathered 'mutism' as if it were common sense, certainly nothing out of the ordinary. Often, I found myself feeling uncomfortably chatty with others. I thought I spoke too much, so many wasted words. With so many unknowns soon enough I became obsessed with teasing the meanings out of everything Mother was doing, even if I wasn't sure why I cared, or what this pursuit might have said about my sanity.

Looking back with what I know now, I'm not sure I could even label either of those acts suicide, and that's the problem isn't it? This reductionist obsession with summing it all up: *this story is about this*. In fact, when I'm quite honest with myself—in a way I have come to believe she meant to teach me to be—I don't know what my life would have been without Mother's all-engrossing mystery to solve. And so, despite the medical spin the doctors put on her mutism after the second time, I was convinced her silence was not only a choice; it was part of her plan. I was right, though it would take me years to understand in what way.

As the story goes, God had created his world in seven days,

beginning with light and then supplementing that with birds, sea creatures, and man; now I pictured Mother creating hers— the way she'd relied upon the best stories to do for her before. But instead of putting *into* words her experience of reality, she was making *from* the words through which she'd always experienced reality, *an entirely new reality.* My mother was a genius none of us could deal with, who'd discovered a wormhole in the universe through which books were the entry. Haha. I know. Believe me, disbelief is natural. I'm not going to try to dissuade you just yet. But that's why I need to *show* you what happened, *show* you what happened before she disappeared, so you'll understand how she did it.

Of course I didn't know this was literally true at the time. She was into books, yes. She was studying something, had clearly dedicated her life to it. But could I have made the leap in belief that putting it all together would have required? Unlikely. Even if I had, I'd have worked out a way to block it out. Instead, as a teenager, I knew reckless attention seeking and intimacy with every Bad Element in town, forging notes and permission slips Mother couldn't be fussed about, long walks to the grocery store with her wallet and a fake note permitting me to use her credit card. But I hadn't the slightest clue what the fuck Mother —the woman I'd spent every day I could remember in awe of— was doing, and my presence didn't seem to make the slightest difference to whatever it was. I was gutted, and she wasn't even gone yet, though she certainly wasn't the Mother she'd been. But she'd changed after the first suicide attempt, too. Why would I pin anything unusual on this subsequent alteration?

It's a big ask to believe in a point where fiction and fact overlap unless you witness it for yourself. It's a ridiculous amount to take in—especially when we're programmed to develop precisely along the opposite logic route: give up make-believe for the real world. But take solace in this: Believers most often begin as disbelievers. I might say it takes one to know one. That's why the *experience* is so important. If I merely *told* the facts of this story, you'd never believe it. *Show, don't tell.* Yes, Mother. For Christ's sake, I get it.

Back then, when it all began, Angie and I lived it, becoming more like sisters than friends, holed up in Mother's giant house crouched over all those books in the secret stairway, behind a false wall off the kitchen, that went nowhere as far as we could tell, and still I couldn't deal with believing it. Plenty of people were there and still couldn't see it. And so, it makes sense that with something like this, in times like these, only the most dramatic methods of proof will do. I believe this is why Mother did what she did.

But after all those years of shredding tissues in the cheap halogen light of the very expensive, very unclaimable, behavioral therapy office, trying to tamp my hope of her return, I told myself I'd never go back to believing. Imagine your worst fear's come true and live with that, is the survival skill I learned those thousands of dollars later—the way to concentrate on the bits of life that allow you to go on living. It's far more difficult than it sounds. And often, dangerous—living each moment as if it not only *may be*, but *is* in fact, your last.

Later, as a mother myself, I swore I'd never risk losing myself in the obsession of false hope again. I wouldn't do that to *my* daughter. But we never quite know what we'll do until we're shoved right up against that brick wall.

ABOUT THE AUTHOR

Dan Noble is a pseudonym for Daniella Brodsky, the Australian/American author of novels across a number of genres, including general fiction, women's fiction, contemporary romance, romantic comedy, chick lit, and YA. When you see the name Dan Noble, you know you're getting a gripping psychological thriller with a brilliant twist. For free books and more, visit Daniella's website to sign up for the Dan Noble mailing list.

Find out more:

www.daniellabrodsky.com
daniella@daniellabrodsky.com

KISS KILL

Copyright © 2016 by Daniella Brodsky

ISBN-13: 978-0-9848513-4-8 (Paperback Edition)

All rights reserved.

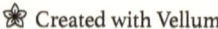 Created with Vellum

THANK YOU FOR READING

If you've enjoyed reading KISS KILL, please share your experience by leaving a review on your website of choice.